The Revelation

Even the book morphs!
Flip the pages
and check it out!

Look for other **ANIMORPHS**®
titles by K.A. Applegate:

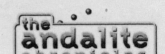

ANIMORPHS®

The Revelation

K.A. Applegate

AN
APPLE
PAPERBACK

SCHOLASTIC INC.
New York Toronto London Auckland Sydney
Mexico City New Delhi Hong Kong

The author wishes to thank Ellen Geroux for her
assistance in preparing this manuscript.

For Michael and Jake

Cover illustration by David B. Mattingly
Art Direction/Design by Karen Hudson/Ursula Albano

ISBN 0-439-11519-1

12 11 10 9 8 7 6 5 4 3 2 1   0 1 2 3 4 5/0

Printed in the U.S.A.
First Scholastic printing, September 2000

CHAPTER 1

My name is Marco.

And I am to cuisine what Sammy Sosa is to baseball.

When it's my night to make dinner, I don't order in. I don't crack open a can of Chef Boyardee and call that a meal. Please.

I go the extra mile.

I use the oven.

I know. You're saying to yourself, "But, Marco, man, you're fighting a war against alien invaders. You and your friends, you guys battle Yeerks twenty-four seven. How do you find the time to cook?!"

It isn't easy. But with a little help from the

1

freezer aisle and a guy I know called Red Baron, it's a lot simpler than it could be.

Plus, this particular night, I was trying to make my stepmom feel, well, glad that she'd married my dad. Even if I wasn't one hundred percent behind the whole thing, she made my dad happy. That's worth something.

A car pulled into the driveway, a car door closed, heels clipped up the sidewalk. Nora, my stepmother.

I threw three paper plates on the table, spread out some silverware, grabbed cups and a block of napkins. Nora doesn't go for paper plates, but hey, it wasn't her night to do the dishes.

The door opened. I heard a sigh, the sound of a heavy bag dropped to the foyer floor.

"Hey," I called.

"Hey," Nora called back. "That faculty meeting lasted far longer than it . . ." The smell of Red Baron's home cooking met her nostrils, no doubt. "Marco!" she cried, entering the kitchen. "You're really making dinner!" She glanced at the paper plates and decided not to comment. "You're the stepson of my dreams."

The woman was a math teacher. I would never really understand her. And now she was going goopy on me.

I forced a smile. "Crazy, isn't it?"

Another car pulled into the drive. Whistling, then rapid steps up the walk.

I grabbed a few sodas from the fridge.

The front door opened. Dad was all spring-in-his-step, a big smile plastered across his face. His cheeks were flushed. He looked like he'd just struck oil.

"Hello, family!"

Okay, that was more enthusiasm than I wanted to see. And the word *family*, when applied to anyone but me, Dad, and my real mom, would always sound very weird. To worsen the nausea, Dad pulled a bouquet of flowers from behind his back.

They were not for me.

I think there was a kiss. Maybe some mushy whispers. I don't know. I looked away. I see enough of the "power of love" between Jake and Cassie, and Rachel and Tobias.

"What's the occasion?" Nora giggled like a middle-schooler and sat at the table.

"Oh, nothing," Dad said, beaming at her from the chair opposite. "You're just the most wonderful woman in the world."

"I know better than that." Her adult voice reemerged as she set the flowers aside. "What's gotten into you?"

"Let's just say things are getting pretty exciting at work. Taking those stock options could be the best thing that ever happened to us."

The buzzer rang. I pulled the pizza from the oven and cut it up on a pizza board.

"What's the big deal, Dad? We gonna be rich?"

I heaped a cheese-dripping slice in front of him.

"Well . . ." he said slowly, "what my team is working on may just be one of the greatest advances in human history."

"An HBO descrambler?"

"Marco, I'm serious. Discoveries like the one we just made make me want to see you do well in math." He looked knowingly at Nora. "Or at least pass an exam."

"He's right. Mathematics is the language of nature. It's the universal language. Everything around us can be represented and understood through numbers." Nora's face had taken on a weird glow. I wondered how numbers could make anyone feel like that.

The nightmare of my last algebra test flashed before my eyes.

"Dad. Just tell us what you're working on."

"I really shouldn't," he said suddenly. "It's secret. Top secret."

Nora gave him a look. It worked.

4

"Okay," Dad said slowly. "If you promise not to say a word . . . and I mean to anybody . . . I guess I can give you the basics."

He swallowed a bite of pizza, then pushed his plate aside so he could lean forward, elbows on the table.

"We've discovered what could be thought of as a whole new dimension, yet not a dimension at all. It's sort of like . . . Marco, you've studied conic sections, haven't you?"

When would I learn not to ask Dad to elaborate? Engineers, like math teachers, have a way of waxing prolific about theoretical situations that put my feeble mind to sleep almost instantly. Even faster than my math book.

"Forget math class," Dad said, realizing that he was losing me. "You know what a cone looks like, right? Well, the surface of a cone is the two-dimensional analogue to the five-dimensional space we inhabit."

I sighed and got up to get another slice. Dad grabbed my arm and made me sit down.

"But a cone is three-dimensional," Nora corrected.

"Exactly. While the surface of the cone is two-dimensional, the surface exists in three dimensions."

"Hmm." Nora seemed perplexed.

"Yeah," I said even louder. "Hmmm."

"The cone contains a singularity," Dad insisted.

"A what?"

"The place where all lines intersect. The place where you can head out in any direction, or in all directions at once. Where you can move in any direction without moving anywhere at all."

"What does this cone have to do with your work?" Nora's puzzled look revealed that Dad had just surpassed her in geekitude. Which, unfortunately, only made him more determined to explain.

"We live our lives on just one line on the cone, in a mere four dimensions, including time."

I felt my eyes rolling up into my head.

"We've been stuck on the surface of the cone all this time. When we want to go anywhere, we have to travel on the line. But now, imagine someone notices the singularity. A point with no size, no breadth, no extent. The physical representation of nothingness. By itself, it's nothing. Yet it's the starting and ending place of everything! A multiplier of real space!"

"Cool," I said. "Look, I've got homework. Lots of math." I dumped my paper plate in the trash and walked into the living room. Flopped on the couch and picked up the remote. I'm an advocate of the quick, pre-homework channel surf.

"What are you calling your discovery?" I heard Nora ask.

"I don't really know," Dad said tentatively. "What can you call something that is nothing at all?"

There wasn't anything on TV. An old *Star Trek*. A new *Star Trek*. My life was plenty sci-fi. How about some *Real World*?

"What could you call it?" Dad continued. "Zero, I suppose. Zero-space."

CHAPTER 2

I almost swallowed a lung.

I sprang up, looked over the couch, stared into the kitchen.

ZERO-SPACE?!

Nora glanced at me with alarm. "Marco, you okay?"

I shut my gaping mouth. Forced myself to blink.

Normal. Be normal. Act normal.

"Fine . . . uh, yeah, um, fine."

I sat back down. My hands were shaking. My head was a rush of adrenaline. How had I missed it! He'd been describing Zero-space. For the past five minutes! How?

How!

I grabbed the cordless and dialed Jake.

"Hello?" he answered.

"We have . . ." I said in a whisper, coughing between words to muffle the sound, "a situation."

There was a pause. I heard a voice in the background, then Jake faking a laugh at one of Tom's wisecracks. Tom, his brother, a Controller. I waited.

Finally, Jake mumbled, "Twenty minutes?"

"Fine," I said, and hung up.

Dad was still talking to Nora. "We're working on a way to communicate through the singularity. Normal matter is dimensional and in theory couldn't pass through."

News flash, Dad: My matter passes through the singularity several times a week. Every time I morph, my excess mass gets sucked into nothingness. A bubble in time.

Dad continued with unchecked enthusiasm. "But we've determined that certain elementary particles could pass through . . ."

I couldn't keep my mouth shut.

I had to know.

If Dad was a Yeerk . . . well, it was simple. I would *not* lose two parents to the enemy.

I *would not.*

"So, Dad," I called, striding back into the kitchen. "You can, like, talk to people through this thing?"

"Precisely," he said.

"How's that any better than a radio?"

I watched his face, his eyes, closer than I ever have. If he was a Controller, I would see it. The Yeerk residue. The arrogance, the conceit. I would see it. You couldn't fight an enemy this long and be helpless to sense its presence, to tell if there's a Yeerk slug wrapped around your own father's brain.

Could you?

"Marco," he said. "Communication through this singularity, through this Zero-space, would be instantaneous. Unlike light, for example, the communication would actually travel zero distance." Dad's eyes were bursting with excitement and wonderment. No evil, no mystery.

"Just think!" he said. "We could talk to the farthest star in an instant, send information faster than the speed of light. No travel distance at all!"

He smiled, certain he'd floored me and Nora both.

"That's fascinating, honey." Her interest, earnest at first, now seemed mostly just polite. She took her bouquet to the sink and began to put the purple buds in water. I sat down in her chair.

"Dad," I said. "When you say you could send communications through this Zero-space thing, what do you mean? I mean, who would you contact? I know there are some fossilized life-forms on Mars, but I don't think they're big on answering the phone."

Dad rocked back in his chair. "Marco, you're a prisoner of your education. They teach you about the solar system. They give you a glimpse of the Milky Way. But do they ever suggest how much is really out there? How many very real chances there are that somewhere beyond our ability to scope, in a place so distant our bodies couldn't hope to live long enough to journey there, life thrives?"

He sounded so innocent. A Yeerk wouldn't let a host go on like that. It just wouldn't.

"What language would you use for the communication?" I probed. "If there's life out there, don't tell me they speak English."

"We could try music," Dad answered easily. "Or math, the universal language." His eyes met Nora's in a look of tender affection.

So pure. So un-Yeerk.

But I needed proof. Proof that he was still just Dad and no one else. Hunches weren't good enough.

"I should get back to the office," he said suddenly, standing up. I stood up next to him.

11

"Higher-ups say that if by the end of the week our team perfects this small device that could, theoretically, send and receive communications through Zero-space, we get to present our findings at next month's conference. You two know what that means . . . ."

Dad grabbed me and Nora around our waists and tried to lift us into the air. Maybe he was a Controller. He'd never done that before.

"It means an all-expenses-paid, bring-your-family-along vacation at an amazing mountain resort. HBO for the boy. Pool time for the wife. Raiding the mini-bar for everyone! We can stay through the weekend. Skip town for five whole days!"

"Five days?" I said.

"If you'd rather go to school . . ."

"No," I said quickly. "It's not that. I just thought . . ." I watched Dad's eyes. "You know, the plants. Five days. That's a long time without Miracle-Gro."

It was a test. Dumb but necessary. If there was a Yeerk in Dad's brain, it wouldn't allow a trip of more than three days. The Kandrona ray feeding cycle is three days. Yeerks aren't flexible on that one.

Dad looked at me like I was an idiot.

"Do you understand what I'm saying? I'm going to pull you out of school. No conic sections.

No biology. My boy, the plants will survive five days." He squeezed Nora's hand. "I've gotta go."

He stopped at the front door. Turned back to us.

"You know what?" he said. "This Zero-space discovery? It's big. Really big. I don't think our lives will ever be the same."

CHAPTER 3

<Impossible!> Ax exclaimed a second time. <There is no way human science can have made such a leap. This is the Yeerks at work.>

"Why would Yeerks use humans to develop a capacity they already have? That's just weird." Rachel looked up from her math book. My ruthless fellow warrior. Rachel isn't content with the whole beauty thing. No, she has to have brains, too. She actually planned to pass the test we had the next day.

We were at Cassie's barn, aka the Wildlife Rehabilitation Center. The place was packed. Vermin of every size and description sprawled out in cages, some scratching, some cawing. Some silent, yet watching.

Ax wasn't in morph. I felt we were vulnerable here, just after dinnertime.

"Are you sure we're safe, Cassie?" I said. She looked up from her math book. I tell you, it was a conspiracy.

"You kidding?" Cassie said. "A PBS documentary on lemurs? A Dome ship could land on the lawn and my parents wouldn't even notice." Cassie's parents are vets, the only people I know who like animals — and animal documentaries — more than Cassie does. "Plus," she continued, nodding toward the red-tailed hawk perched in the hayloft, "we've got Tobias."

<This Z-space thing has to be a trap,> Tobias said. <A very elaborate trap.>

"Too elaborate," I shot back. "Do you really think the Yeerks would go to the trouble of planting the seed of Z-space technology in some piddling human engineering firm? Then wait for humans to pick up on it? And wait even longer for news of the development to leak out and reach us? That's slow and uncertain. Not Yeerk."

"It could be simpler than we think," Jake said calmly, lowering himself onto a bale of hay. This war had aged my best friend in ways you couldn't really see. But you could definitely tell that in his mind he was no longer just a kid. None of us were. "Maybe there's no Z-space device at all. The Yeerks could have put out a rumor, knowing

15

it would draw the Andalite bandits like bees to honey."

"A rumor?" Cassie said doubtfully.

<It has to be,> Ax declared. <There is simply no way that humans are on the verge of Zero-space communications.>

<If human engineers are part of the Yeerk plan,> Tobias reasoned, <that means Marco's dad . . .>

"No." I stood up and began to pace. "The Yeerks don't have my father. They don't. Sure, it looks bad. But he's not a Controller. I tested him. I told you."

"Maybe he fooled you with that five-day trip stuff," Rachel said. "If he knew you were testing him, he would have played along. Outsmarted you at your own game."

"No!" I said firmly, stopping in my tracks. "Look, maybe he's a dupe. Maybe he's an innocent member of the Yeerkish team at the office. But he's not one of them. At least, not yet."

But it suddenly struck me as absurd. He had to be next on the list. Where was he right that minute? At the office, like he'd told us? Or at the Yeerk pool? And why . . . why had they let him stay free this long? Did the Yeerks need a buffer, a genuinely ignorant human to keep their cover strong?

Or had they just been waiting for the right opportunity to seize and infest him? Like tonight.

<You must admit,> Ax said solemnly, <it is unlikely the Yeerks would set a trap, yet leave one member of their team uncontrolled. It would be an enormous security breach.>

I felt Jake's eyes on me, then his hand on my shoulder.

"How do we handle this, Marco? Your dad, your call."

Jake is a diplomatic leader. He makes it a policy to ask for input. But what I really wanted right then was dictatorship. I wanted him to order us to save my father.

"I don't know," I said instead. "What about a stakeout at Dad's office? He's there now."

Jake glanced at Cassie. "Okay," he said. "A stakeout, starting now. Ax and Tobias, stick with Marco's dad until he leaves the office and gets home."

That's when I realized why Jake had looked at Cassie. Jake had asked her if she thought I could be trusted. He said it all in one quick glance.

And she'd said no.

They thought I was too close to this. Poor Marco was about to lose a second parent to the enemy. Of course he'd snap.

"Marco," Jake continued, "you keep watch on the homefront. I'll check with Erek to see what he knows. We'll compare notes in the morning."

Ax morphed to northern harrier and flapped up toward Tobias.

"I want to go with them," I said. "It's more likely the Yeerks will try to infest Dad away from home."

"They'll take care of it," Jake said. "They don't have a stepmother waiting for them to come home. Nothing's gonna happen without you."

Did he mean it? Something in his tone made me wonder.

"You can't be sure of that, Jake. What if something does happen? I want to be there."

"You will be. Just go home for now. Everything's gonna be cool." He smiled, but it didn't reach his eyes.

I walked out of the barn and started down the road. I didn't morph to bird. I wanted to walk as a kid. I wanted to pretend for just a minute that a kid was all I was.

But my mind knew better.

Jake, my oldest friend, didn't trust me to do the right thing when family was involved.

I would show him he was wrong.

CHAPTER 4

Brrrrrrring!

I jolted from sleep like a SAC pilot at the alarm. Ready to run to my plane . . . start up, take off, fight!

Wait. No, it was the phone. And I was Marco, the kid who'd fallen asleep over his math book. There was drool on the page. Gross.

Brrrrrrring!

I reached for the phone on my desk. I lifted it up and was about to say . . .

"Hello?" Dad said in a groggy voice. We'd picked up at the same time. Dad hadn't noticed.

"It's Jack, from work."

"Jack. Hey. What can I do for you?"

The call was for Dad, who was home, alive, and in bed. I could hang up. Should hang up. I looked at my watch. Eleven P.M. Why was someone from work calling so late?

"It's Russ," said the flat male voice. "There's been a car accident. Russ is dead."

"Oh, God!"

"Russ's wife is . . . she's hysterical, she's . . . you know what it's like. You lost a spouse. We thought you'd be best at comforting her. Can you swing by her place?"

"Sure," Dad said.

I hung up the phone. Heard Dad head downstairs, still on the line, getting the widow's address.

I'd met Russ at a company picnic a few years ago. I'd met his wife, too. My mind flashed to the night Mom disappeared, to the terror that wound around my heart when I realized she was never coming home.

"Hmph," I said aloud. "Sad."

I looked back at my math. Problem 8. I squinted at it. Totally incomprehensible no matter how you looked at it. Problem 9 . . .

It hit me. A flash, a surge of insight. Puzzle pieces dropping into place. Not problem 9, but the phone call.

A guy from work had been killed, a guy working on the Z-space project. A call late at night. A voice on the phone saying, "We thought you'd be best at comforting her."

We?

"Oh, God!"

I jumped up, flung open the bedroom door. The electric garage door banged lightly closed. Dad's car pulling out!

No.

He was driving into a trap and I hadn't listened long enough to get the address.

I sailed down the stairs three at a time. Checked the notepad by the cordless. Nothing. The notepad on Dad's desk. Nothing again.

Where was Russ's house?

Where would "they" be waiting?

His computer screen was still up — no screensaver. At the bottom was a minimized "window," the words *Yahoo! Maps* written inside. I grabbed the mouse and clicked.

Bingo — 1366 Fairmont and a road map in case I planned to drive. I didn't.

I was going to fly. But I had to call in backup first.

I dialed Jake, punching numbers frantically as I walked toward the back door.

"Hello?" It wasn't Jake. The voice was gruff and hoarse. It was Tom.

I hung up instantly. The phone rang in my hand and before I could think, I answered.

21

"Who is this? You just called and hung up on me. Who is this!" Tom had finally discovered *69.

I was shaken up, embarrassed. I pictured the Yeerk on the other end of the line. "It's Marco," I muttered. "I wanted to talk to Jake. Sorry."

Tom grunted into the phone and hung up.

So much for Jake. Who else was there? Ax, Tobias. They were back in the woods. Cassie's parents would be in the way. Rachel.

I dialed. She picked up.

"Do you want to hang out?" I said. Always speak in code. Always be careful.

"Where?"

"Thirteen sixty-six Fairmont."

"When?"

"Five minutes ago."

"What we talked about earlier?"

"Uh-huh."

I set the phone down and headed for the door. I was glad Rachel was the one. If you think a situation could get ugly, you want Rachel on your side.

"Marco?" Nora, standing half-asleep on the stairs. "Where's your father?"

"Dad? He just ran to the store. Probably had a craving for Chunky Monkey. He'll be back soon."

Nora considered for a moment, seemed to buy it, and went back to bed.

I headed out the door. I morphed to osprey in the backyard. It was dangerous, but it was dark. I started flapping hard before my wings had fully formed.

Up and up and up. The streetlights reduced the night city to a simple grid. The Yahoo! map.

I swooped down, lower and lower, until I spotted Dad's car.

Already there!

I dove like a stunt plane. Demorphed in the bushes.

Lights were on in the house's lower level. Dense, red curtains shielded the windows. Shadows played on the fabric. Strange silhouettes, sudden movements. A struggle.

Where was Rachel?! I edged toward the house, crawl-walking to keep my head below the hedge. I stopped at a side window. Pressed my face to a place where the curtain didn't quite meet the window's edge.

"Ahhh!" A distorted voice from somewhere in the room.

Two Hork-Bajir stood rigid guard. Beyond them, two human-Controllers wrestling my father into a chair . . . tying him down . . . securing him next to a portable Yeerk pool!

One of the men was Russ. The "dead" guy was alive.

I stood up. Forget about caution and stealth

23

and security. *Forget about everything except Dad,* instinct said.

Still, I stood, immobile. Watched as one of the men pushed my father's head down to the edge of the tank. Dad struggled, a desperate paroxysm of terror. The man slapped him across the face.

Dad kicked the pool. Fluid spilled over the edge, onto the carpet.

I watched, fascinated. Was this real? Was this now?

Then anger and hate reared up like demons inside of me.

"This can't happen," I said quietly. "Not Dad. Not again . . ."

Instinct ordered me to end the nightmare, lunge through the glass, destroy the Controllers, free my father.

But you're an Animorph, my rational mind argued. *A soldier. You have to let it happen. You can't save him now. Even temporary freedom would mean the end. The Yeerks won't stop till they find him. Find you. Your friends. You have to let it happen. It's the smart thing to do. The only thing to do.*

I watched. Dad's head was forced into the sludge. One eye sunk beneath the surface. The other fixed in horror on the slug that was swimming closer. Closer. Closer . . .

CHAPTER 5

"Noooooo!"

I raised a huge, black fist to break the glass. I had morphed, without realizing or willing it.

Gorilla: my outward expression of an inner rage too great to contain.

That was it. This was the end of smart. And the beginning of right.

Crash!

I broke the glass and pulled myself through the shattered window. A million sparkling fragments rained to the floor. Cool night air rushed in behind me. The red curtains flapped frantically.

Everyone froze. All eyes. On me.

I seized the nearest object, a huge oak chair, and flung it out of my path. Gorilla arms are like heavy machinery. You think, *I'll move that,* and it just happens. No straining. No effort.

The chair smashed and splintered into a mirror on the wall. This breaking glass thing, it was becoming my calling card.

<Step away from the pool and you might not get hurt,> I bellowed.

"Andalite," the "dead" man spat.

The two Hork-Bajir guards lunged. Rushed for me around either side of the dark leather couch, leg blades shredding upholstery as they passed.

I grabbed the closest weapon, the glass globe from a floor lamp. <Heads up!> I sneered, and threw the globe like a fast ball. One of the Hork-Bajir fumbled it like a hot potato. Fell backward and hit his head on a table. These goons were not pro-ball material.

<You. At the table. Get your head up!> I yelled to Dad, faking a voice deeper than my own. <Get it above the surface. Now!>

I saw him tilt his neck, strain against an angry human hand.

The base of the lamp was still in my fist, a long wrought-iron pole.

Whack! Whack! Whack!

I quickly struck the second Hork-Bajir in the knees, in the stomach, in the head. He fell to the ground. A thud, then a clatter.

I heaved the couch aside.

My father yelled again. I turned to see his head slip back into the pool! Sludgy slime lap against his cheek!

And a Yeerk slug began to slither into his ear!

<NO!>

It was maybe the weirdest moment I'll ever live. In an instant, everything changed. Live action became slow motion. I saw Dad's future in my hands.

My hands alone.

I charged forward, arm extended, hand outstretched. Slow . . . too slow!

"Ahhhh!"

Yes! I caught the slug's slippery back half in my massive fingers and yanked it out of my father's head. Slapped it to the floor.

The human-Controller backed off. I grabbed the chair in which my father was tied and slid it across the floor, into the wall. He cursed and kicked, still tied down. But he was free. That was all that mattered.

I wrapped my hands around the edge of the mini-pool and heaved.

A hundred gallons of Kandronal fluid slopped onto the floor. One solitary gray Yeerk floated away in the torrent. It knocked against the leg of a side table and was swept toward the glass patio doors. Just as it was about to smack into the track at the base of the doors, I slid them open. The fluid drained quickly onto the deck outside.

There was a soft splat as the Yeerk dropped over the edge.

<The opposition has been crushed,> I said to the people who remained standing. I took a step toward them and what was left of their confidence. They'd seen me take two Hork-Bajir out of commission. They knew I could rip their arms from their sockets.

I took another step — and their expressions changed. They smiled with identical half-grins. It didn't make sense. Not until I realized they weren't looking at me.

SSSSEEEWW! SSSSEEEWW!

Twin blades screamed toward my neck! Two new Hork-Bajir!

I ducked but the sabers grazed my head. I hit the floor. Scampered under the diningroom table. Both Hork-Bajir were right behind me. I shoved a chair in their path. One of them kicked it away.

I dove for an overstuffed armchair, gripped the legs, and threw it behind me to block them. They fought with the cotton batting and foam just long enough for me to leap over the destroyed couch and hoist it into the air! Turn it on them like a battering ram!

<Ahhhh!>

I grunted. Heaved.

I hoped Russ had homeowner's insurance.

Ka-plash! Bam!

I missed both Hork-Bajir, but made a bull's-eye with the entertainment center.

One of the Hork-Bajir began to laugh. At least I think that's what he was doing.

I backed up and hit the wall. They stomped toward me, blades flying, beak-mouths open. Whoa. Seriously hazardous breath.

I looked up. Down. Left, right. There had to be an escape route. Some domestic weapon I hadn't used!

A Hork-Bajir claw squeezed my neck and pushed me back.

I gasped for air and tried punching for his stomach. Couldn't reach. My face scrunched up with pain, head started to swirl . . .

<It's been fun, boys,> I panted. <But now I have to go home.>

They had exactly one second to think I was crazy.

"Rooooooaaaaarrrrr!"

Gigantic paws, armed with claws that can gut a salmon before you can say "lox," knocked their heads together.

I don't even want to describe what Rachel

29

did next. Let's just say those particular Yeerks wouldn't trouble anyone for a while.

<Nice of you to show,> I huffed, falling back against the wall, blood smearing on the paint.

<Looks like I'm a little late,> Rachel answered, turning her weak grizzly eyes on Dad.

CHAPTER 6

Dad had never looked as terrified as he did at that moment. He was really pale. Paper-white. He was trembling.

Weeeeeeeoooooo! Weeeeeeeeoooooo!

Sirens screamed in the distance. They were coming for us. I stepped forward. Dad cowered like he expected me to kill him.

Marco, you idiot, you're a freakin' gorilla! Speak to him, say something. Get him to trust you.

<We're here to help you,> I said trying to disguise my voice. <It's okay.> Dad's eyes darted from the ape to the bear, not nearly convinced.

<Great,> Rachel said privately. <Now what? What are we supposed do with him?>

31

<He's seen way too much. Obviously, the Yeerks mean to make everyone involved in the Z-space research a Controller. Now that Dad's been saved by an Andalite bandit, there's no way out for him.>

I paused, looking at the totaled living room. What had I done? I was insane. This whole thing was insane. <I think, maybe, it's time . . .>

I waited for Rachel to answer. She was silent. I took it as a sign that she agreed.

<One thing's for sure,> she said suddenly. <You SO have to get out of here!>

I lurched forward, untied Dad, and grabbed him around the waist. He tensed and fought, hollered desperately.

<Listen up!> I growled. <We're the good guys. We're all you've got.>

He kicked one more time, then settled. I dragged him out through the patio door, through the ankle-deep Yeerk sludge. Rachel followed. We lumbered for Dad's parked car. I released him in front of the driver's door.

<Get in!>

I ran to the passenger's side and grabbed the door. Whoops! Too hard. It ripped almost completely off the hinges.

<What are you doing?!> Rachel snorted.

I shrugged, jammed my body into the cab,

and slid the seat back all the way, which made absolutely no difference. My head curled toward the dash. A leg and an arm hung out the broken-door side of the car.

Police car tires screeched around the corner at the intersection that had to be about five blocks back. Some of the police were free, but most were Controllers. Why bet on which kind was coming?

Dad fumbled with the keys like an old man. His breath came fast and shallow.

<Where are you going to go?> Rachel asked. <How are we going to find you?>

<I'll let you know as soon as I can,> I said. The engine choked to life. Rachel backed into the bushes.

Police streamed down the street.

<DRIVE!> I bellowed. <MOVE!> Dad was too scared not to obey. We pulled out as the flashing lights and white sedans shrieked to a halt at 1366. I looked back through the door hole.

<Rachel?> I called into the darkness, not sure if she could hear me. <Thanks.>

A van cruised past the squad cars and sped on toward us.

<Come on! Let's move!>

We crept along with a traumatized man at the wheel. Dad turned onto the street that would take us home.

<No!> I yelled.

"But . . . my son," he gasped. "My wife."

<South! Step on it!> I ordered. <You can't go home.>

I couldn't let him. Impossible. Too dangerous. Nora was probably already in Yeerk hands . . .

The van slammed us from behind. Whiplash threw our heads back. I looked over my shoulder. Two Hork-Bajir were in the cab. Another one hung out the sliding side door. Inside, I could only guess. Six or seven or more.

<Crap!>

Dad only gaped in terror.

<We're being followed. Come on! Get to the highway!> But he was frozen up. I had to take control.

I grabbed the wheel. Stretched and punched my massive foot onto the gas, right on top of Dad's shoe.

Skreeeeeee!

We took off like a Formula One.

"Ahhhh!" Dad yelled. Either I'd smashed his foot or my driving was even worse than I thought.

The Yeerks were stuck to our tail. I ran a red light, swerved onto an exit ramp, merged into highway traffic.

Or tried to . . .

Horns screamed obscenities. I did feel a little

bad about grazing the Jeep Cherokee. And that Dodge. And the Honda.

But we weren't losing the van!

I moved left one lane. Two lanes. Three lanes. Four lanes.

The van was still glued to our bumper!

A sign. Exit 54 . . .

Scrrrrrreeeeeeekkk! I braked, tires burning the pavement.

Swerved across four lanes of traffic, from the far-left lane to the exit ramp.

Screeeeeeek! The Yeerks followed.

<Take the wheel!> I ordered. He did.

I looked back. The Yeerks had turned too sharply. They were tipping . . . tipping . . . skidding toward the concrete divider . . .

Kaaachoomp! A terrific crash as we drove out of sight.

There are bad drivers, and there are worse drivers.

The residential neighborhood was quiet, asleep. It was after midnight and the sky was starless. Eventually, we turned onto a two-lane back road.

"Who are you?" Dad said, pushing on the brakes and pulling onto the shoulder. "What are you?"

<Remember those bladed guys who were try-

35

ing to kill me? About two hundred of them are looking for us right now. If you don't keep driving . . .>

The car stopped. Dad opened the door. Threw himself out and started to run.

<No!> I yelled.

He tumbled into the drainage ditch, got up, and took off across a field of tall grass.

I yanked myself out of the car and loped after him. There was only one thing to do. But all I could think about was the last person who'd been in the know, the last person who'd discovered the Animorphs' secret.

He'd ended up trapped as a rat. Forever. We'd done it to him. We'd had to.

<Dad!> I called in thought-speak. In the voice that was my own.

He froze. Turned. Looked back at me.

In the glow of the car headlights, I began to demorph. To slowly transform from beast to boy right before my father's eyes.

Dad stood still as a statue, eyes wide. As my body took shape, I saw tears start to well in his eyes.

"It's me," I said as soon as my human mouth formed.

Dad gasped huskily. Stepped toward me through the grass. "How? I don't understand."

He touched my hair, my face, my shoulders. Then he grabbed me. Hugged me. The tears on his cheek dripped onto my own.

"How?" he said again.

"It's a long story, Dad. A really long story."

CHAPTER 7

We ordered burgers from an all-night diner on the outskirts of town. The place was too much of a dump for the Yeerks to check out. I hoped. I made us eat in the car anyway, in a dark corner of the parking lot.

I told Dad everything. Almost.

My story seemed to wash over him somehow. He looked stunned, disbelieving. He shook his head as though everything I was telling him was, well, just too much for the man.

When I stopped talking, the first thing he said was that he had to call Nora.

I let him walk across the gravel parking lot to the pay phone. Let him dial the numbers.

"Honey, it's me," he said. "Yeah, I'm okay."

I could hear Nora on the other end. Yelling, worried, scared.

"I'm with Marco," Dad said. "Where? We're at the . . ."

I cut the connection and grabbed the receiver from Dad's ear. Slammed it down angrily.

He glared at me. "What was that?" he demanded.

For the first time since the brutality at Russ's house, it felt like the father I knew was with me. Real Dad. Thinking Dad. Authority-figure Dad. For the first time since I'd demorphed, the look in his eye was anything but distant.

"Why did you do that?"

I started to walk back to the car. He followed.

"I said, what was that about!"

I sat down on the passenger car seat. Dad got in his side and slammed the door. He had a door to slam.

"You know exactly what it was about," I said calmly. "If you've been listening to me at all, you know that by now the Yeerks have staked out our house, probably tapped our phone. I'd bet they're sitting on our couch right now, waiting for you to walk in the door so they can —"

"Stop," Dad said angrily. "Stop it. I've listened to you. I've heard every word. But you have to understand . . . I have no proof, no . . . how can I believe all these things you say? You

39

changed from a gorilla into my son. But I only think I saw that. I was terrified. I was tortured, then kidnapped. Maybe my mind is making things up. Maybe this is a dream."

Before he'd finished talking, I was on my way.

My skin hardened, then blackened, then thinned like eggshell. Legs and arms shortened until there was nothing left to hold me up. I fell forward onto the seat, shrinking and shrinking until the crumbs from the burger bun looked like boulders, and then blindness cut my view.

Shloooooop!

My waist reduced to millimeters, splicing me almost in half.

"Oh, God!" Dad cried. "Oh, no!"

I was becoming an ant. But I wasn't going to wait for the ant's mind to surface. No.

I began to demorph.

I let Dad watch me and all the horror and weirdness of morphing. I let Dad sit there, alone and up close with his new reality, as I demorphed back to boy. And began to morph again.

Feathers imprinted my skin in 2-D, then 3-D. They grew up and out as my body shrank and my head deformed. My nose grew hard and sharp and hooked. My fingers, though smaller, grew stronger, became flesh-piercing talons. Eyes sharpened to superhuman clarity.

Again, I started the return trip to boy. Back to the form Dad knew as his son.

"I have about twenty other animals I could morph to," I said as the last feather disappeared. "Want to see my lobster?"

A cold sweat coursed in tiny rivulets down the side of my father's head. He didn't need to see any more.

I'd scared him, creeped him out. Made him nervous and worried and concerned. He was handling it. For a guy whose reality had just been completely rocked, he was handling it pretty well.

He looked out through the windshield and stared for a moment at a point far away. The sun was just beginning to think about rising. It gave our desolate patch of the world a preview. Dad looked back at me.

"I get it," he said slowly. "I get it. You've been through hell."

"Through hell and back." I smiled. "A few times."

Dad smiled back.

"I'm going to take you to some friends of mine, Dad," I said. "You can hang out with them until we decide . . ."

"Whoa," Dad said quickly. "Are you nuts? I'm going to the police."

"Dad, the Yeerks are the police. I can't let you do that."

He was shocked and confused again. "What do you mean you can't let me? *I'm* your father. I tell *you* what to do."

Not in this reality, Dad. Not in this world.

"Dad, of course you're my father," I said, fighting an onslaught of emotion. *And it would be so nice to have someone make decisions for me again,* I added silently. "I love you. I respect you. But I've been fighting this war for a long time. I've been on more missions, in more fights, and seen more terrible things than you can imagine. This is my fight. My war. Me and my friends, we know what's going on. You don't."

Dad frowned at me, then looked back at the rising sun.

"You've told me what's going on," he said quietly.

"Not everything. I left something out."

Dad chuckled sardonically. "Let me guess. Visser Three's your father, your mother's an Andalite, and I'm no relation at all."

"No," I said. No way around it. My fingers gripped the vinyl of the seat. "Mom's not an Andalite. And she didn't drown. She's the host to Visser One. The Yeerk who started the invasion of Earth. Mom's been the visser's slave since before she disappeared."

Dad's face went white. "You mean Eva?"

"I mean Mom."

Dad bent forward. His head hit the steering wheel. His hands pressed into his face.

"Oh, God," he said.

"She's alive."

"I didn't know . . ."

He rocked back against the seat. His head hit the headrest. "If only I'd waited . . ." He covered his eyes, then uncovered them. Then he reached for the glove box, rifled through, and pulled out a pack of cigarettes and a lighter. He stuck one in his mouth and made it burn.

"Dad, what are you doing?" I said nicely. "You stopped five years ago. Cut it out."

Dad looked at me and threw the cigarette out the window.

"I love Nora," he said. "I love her as much as I loved your mother."

The words made my throat tighten. He didn't. Couldn't. Nora was nice, but . . . she was a math teacher.

My mother was everything.

But he loved Nora. Somehow, that was news to me.

Fatigue and light-headedness struck me like a steel beam. My head was spinning. The rising sun seemed cruel and inappropriate.

"I'm going to take you to some friends of

43

mine," I said quietly. "Drive us back toward the city."

My mother was in the hands of the enemy. I felt like I was the only one who cared.

Dad loved this other woman.

I wished I'd kept my mouth shut.

My universe, my dreams, were falling apart.

CHAPTER 8

We got off the highway at an exit not far from our house. But we weren't going home.

It was six A.M. Rush hour had already begun. Who knew people left their houses that early? Rolling out of bed in time for school is torture enough for me.

Dad's stubble made him look rough, but he was holding on. Finding out about Mom had done something funny to his face. It was stiff and hard. Different.

"Turn here," I said. "It's the third house on the right."

The houses in the subdivision were all new and big and similar-looking, with two-car garages at the end of every driveway.

"The one with the black Lab taking a leak on the lawn?"

"Uh-huh."

We parked the car, walked up the path, and rang the bell. I eyed the street as we waited. The van of Hork-Bajir was a vivid memory. I watched as a car pulled out of a garage across the street and drove away.

I heard Erek coming to the door.

"Dad, it's about to get weird."

"Please," Dad said calmly. "It can't get any weirder."

"Dad, just a suggestion, but when you're dealing with the Animorphs, never say it can't get any weirder. It always does."

Erek King — Erek the Chee — opened the door.

"Uh-oh," he said, looking from Dad to me.

"Yeah, I know," I said.

"Does he?" Erek asked with alarm.

I nodded. Erek grabbed our arms and pulled us inside. The door slammed and bolted behind us. We stood in Mr. King's living room, the facade of normalcy that masked the expansive, rambling, underground Chee dog park. Just feet below where we stood.

Dad's eyes trained to the couch. Then his mouth dropped open. He stumbled back against the wall.

Mr. King sat on the couch, watching the *Today* show. Normal enough. Only thing was he didn't have clothes on. No skin, either. He was relaxing *au naturel*, which for him meant lounging as an android. No human hologram.

When Mr. King realized Dad was about to lose it, his hologram shimmered instantly into place.

"The Chee, remember?" I said. "An ancient android race created by the Pemalites and hard-wired for peace. I told you all about them."

"Right," Dad said weakly. "I just thought you were pulling my leg."

"Erek," I said, "the Yeerks are after my dad. With a little Yeerk information, Dad here went and invented a Z-space transponder. Then he made them really mad when he broke away before they could get a slug in his ear. Can you hide him here without violating your programming? And can you disappear his car right away?"

"No problem," Erek said. "Of course he can stay. Does he like dogs?"

Dad glanced at me. We had roughly the same feelings for Nora's dog, Euclid. Annoyance and pity mixed with a very small, almost nonexistent, amount of affection. But then, Nora's dog was hardly what you'd call a real dog.

"I love them," Dad said, faking a laugh.

"Erek," I said, "there's one other thing. Dad's missing. And that means that every aspiring sub-visser in the metro area is looking for a lead. I'm a lead. If I turn up missing, too . . . if they think we've both disappeared . . ."

"They'll go after your friends."

"This do-do is pretty deep, isn't it?"

"Yeah, but we'll handle it," Erek said. "Don't worry. We'll give the Yeerks just what they want to see: you and your dad, alive and well and seemingly clueless." Before our eyes, Erek altered his programming to become an exact duplicate of Dad.

"Did he, uh, morph me?" Dad said, stunned.

"No. Remember, Erek's an android. And that's a hologram."

"Oh," Dad said, suddenly getting it. "Oh, wow." The engineer in him had just kicked in. Technical curiosity brought him back to life. He reached out to touch Erek's hologram. His hand went right through the "skin."

"Whoa!" he cried. "Unbelievable! Erek, you have to tell me about the rendering process. I want to know everything." He pulled his hand out, then stuck it inside again, this time at waist level.

Erek frowned like Dad was infringing on his dignity, but he was polite about it. "We'll talk later," he said, gently removing Dad's hand from his hologram guts.

"Right," Dad said, embarrassed. "So, you're able to project holograms of me and Marco? What about Nora? Someone has to look out for her."

Erek and I exchanged glances. He knew as well as I that we were probably too late.

"We'll do everything in our power," Erek said. "But you have to realize the Yeerks move fast. You should prepare for the worst."

I looked at my father's pained, exhausted face and my stomach sank. I risked my life almost every day on all sorts of crazy missions, and yet I'd chosen not to go back for Nora. Now she was probably beyond help and it was my fault.

I decided Dad wasn't ready for the truth.

"They won't touch her," I lied. "She's at school most of the day. Everything will be fine."

Dad looked comforted.

"Come with me," Erek said, replacing the hologram of Dad with the one I knew, a boy about Jake's size. We headed for the stairs. I pulled Erek aside.

"You know the Yeerks may not waste time trying for another infestation with Dad. They'll most likely just try to kill him. What if they shoot you?"

"I can resist low-power attack by Dracon beams."

"But what about full power?"

Erek shrugged. "It'll depend on the angle, the duration, and blind luck. Marco, my programming only forbids me to use violence, even in the best of causes. It doesn't forbid me to die."

"Yeah, well, I do."

We followed Dad down the narrow stairs to the basement. Then, just like I remembered, the floor began to drop like an elevator. Five floors down it stopped and the wall before us disappeared into a golden hallway of light.

Then we were in the vast, glowing chamber. The grass underfoot extended for yards. Streams cut across the grass and wildflowers dotted the banks. Butterflies and bees inspected the flowers, and squirrels scampered up and down the various kinds of trees.

And throughout the entire park hundreds, maybe even thousands, of happy, healthy dogs ran and played, watched over by a handful of muzzle-mouthed Chee in android form.

"These are the Chee," Erek explained to Dad. "They'll be good to you while you stay."

Dad sank down on the grass, under a tree. Two or three tail-wagging doggies ran up to greet him. A mid-sized mutt started licking his face and kept licking until Dad agreed to pet her.

"You'll take good care of him?" I said to Erek. I glanced back at Dad and saw that his eyes were closed. He was falling asleep with the mutt still licking his face. Two doglike Chee approached. One put a pillow under my father's head. The other covered him with a blanket.

Erek smiled. "I think he'll be okay."

CHAPTER 9

I was the last to arrive at the barn. Rachel quickly looked away when I met her glance. So, she'd already told the others.

Tobias glared at me with his intense hawk eyes. The others weren't much more friendly.

"Go ahead," I said, my voice not quite steady. "You can say it. I'm crazy. Stupid. IN-SANE!"

Silence. What could I expect? I'd shown Jake that he was right not to trust me. I'd done just what he was afraid I would do.

I hadn't done the right thing.

I'd let emotions get in the way of reason.

And I wasn't any happier about it than my friends were.

"There's no excuse," I said now, "but here's

what happened. One second I vowed to let the Yeerks infest my father. The next second I was battling a dozen Hork-Bajir."

<Rachel said there were four,> Ax said.

"Whatever."

"Do you have any idea what this means?" Jake asked calmly.

"Of course." I looked at the others, then back at Jake. "It means no more math tests." No one smiled. I sat down on a block of hay and put my head in my hands, a head vibrating from fatigue. I just wanted to lie down.

"I know," I said. "I'm sorry."

"It's okay, Marco," Cassie said kindly. "No one ever said it was easy for you. I know I couldn't . . . I couldn't sit by and watch the Yeerks take my parents."

"And you shouldn't," Rachel said fiercely. "Cassie's right. Marco acted like a human being." She paused. "There's a first time for everything."

<The action was imprudent,> Ax said, concern in his alien face. <You acted alone and publicly.>

<The Yeerks will track down everyone connected to your dad,> Tobias echoed. <Starting with you. Ending with the rest of us.>

"I'm a step ahead of you, Bird-boy," I said wearily. "Erek and I have a plan for that."

"We can't go back in time. What's done is done," Jake said philosophically. "The point now is that we know the Z-space device exists."

"And we have to get it!" Rachel.

I shook my head. "Mission impossible. If the Yeerks have made Controllers of everyone at the lab, if they know we're going to try for the device, it's suicide. And for what?"

"If we get our hands on that thing, we have a megaphone to the universe," Rachel replied. "An interplanetary cell phone."

<I believe the device would require more than a single lithium-ion battery,> Ax said practically.

"You know what I mean. I'm talking about communication with the forces that matter. Direct communication with the Andalite fleet."

<Not if we're dead,> Tobias muttered.

Rachel heaved a sigh. Cassie looked at her.

"From the last reports we got," Cassie said, "Earth is not an Andalite priority. What good will it do to contact a fleet that can't help us? Or doesn't want to?"

"We're not sure how things stand," I countered. "None of our information is firsthand."

Rachel stood up, aggravated by a lack of initiative.

"What's the matter with you guys? Don't you realize that a Z-space transponder means access to all Z-space transmissions? Isn't that right, Ax?"

<Yes.>

"So, it's not just a way to phone home," Rachel argued. "It's a chance to *intercept* Yeerk transmissions."

I felt like an idiot for not having seen it before.

How often do you get a chance at interplanetary surveillance? A chance to bug a Yeerk telephone?

<I . . .> Ax hesitated, began to pace, then spoke again. <This human-made device is, seemingly at least, equal to or even superior . . .> I swear he was trying to stop himself from choking on the words. <. . .superior to Yeerk technology.>

"Look," I said. "Whatever this device is, however complicated it is, it was built with man-made components, right?"

Ax looked increasingly annoyed.

<It took Andalites three millennia to breach the confines of the home world with a simple combustion rocket. Our race matured greatly before Z-space was discovered. We were ready for the challenges. We were prepared for zero-dimensional travel and communication.>

"I know, Ax," I said. "Humans are absurd and immature. But you're missing my point. If the device was built with man-made components, my dad should be able to re-create it."

This time, a definite choking sound.

"I mean, you should be able to re-create it. Dad could help." The amended statement seemed acceptable to Ax.

Jake nodded.

"Ax?"

<I will do it, Prince Jake.>

"Well, then," Jake said, "let's go for it. This is too important not to try."

CHAPTER 10

Ax and I fell into a gentle dive over the blocks of indistinguishable subdivision houses, until bamm! We were right over Erek's.

A moment later we landed in the wildly thick grass between the pool house and a row of shrubs. For the first time it occurred to me that if the Chee can't wage war on individuals, maybe they're also prevented from harming the environment any more than is necessary to maintain their cover. Lawn fertilizer as environmental insult.

<This grass is delicious,> Ax said, demorphing in the cover of trees and grinding a newly formed hoof into the weeds. <Fresh and tasty.>

I might have made a witty comment, but my

57

mouth was exactly halfway between osprey beak and fleshy human lips. An impediment to fluid conversation.

Ax morphed to human and together we trudged through the grass to the back door.

"This is called a patio," Ax observed. "Paddy. Paddy-ohhhh."

"Uh-huh. And this is the patio door. Come on."

The kitchen was clean and bright. I walked through to the living room. Absolutely normal-looking with a couch, chairs, knickknacks. A TV playing on mute. A clip of the president talking to high school students.

"That TV's been on for a year now," I said.

I turned to head downstairs. Ax wasn't behind me.

"Ax?"

No answer. Just a crunching sound in the kitchen.

I backtracked. The refrigerator door was open. I peered over the top.

The Chee are very hospitable. Milk and cookies were waiting for us in the fridge. Ax had decided it was snack time.

"Orr-ee-oohh!" he said, looking at me wide-eyed. Brown crumbs and frosting covered his chin.

"Come on!" I ordered.

"ORR-EE-OHH . . ."

Sometimes it's easy to forget the boy is a warrior.

Downstairs, we found Erek waiting for us near the entrance to Dog Park World.

"Where's my dad?" I asked, looking around a little nervously. In the back of my mind was the fear that Dad would decide to leave and rescue Nora. The Chee would be powerless to stop him.

But Erek pointed to a tree in a far corner of the brilliantly glowing park.

"He's right over here . . ."

Dad was reclining peacefully, several dogs curled up at his side. When he saw me, he mouthed "shhhh" and motioned to a sleeping puppy.

He seemed relaxed. Almost too relaxed. Maybe he'd faced his new reality. Maybe he'd simply blocked it out.

"Listen, Dad," I whispered over the puppy. "Me and my friends need your help. Your work on the Z-space transponder might be the most important thing that's ever happened to us. It could change everything."

"I think I said those exact words yesterday," he said wistfully.

"Could you build it again, Dad?"

The question seemed to shake him from his dream world. He sat up abruptly and the dogs scattered.

"But I'd need to be back in the lab," Dad continued. "All my calculations . . . the equipment and instruments, not to mention the components. It would be impossible without going back there."

"We cannot permit you to return to the lab," Ax stated flatly. "The Yeerks control it now. They will be waiting for you. I am well versed in Z-space field theory. I can help . . . I can help you build the device."

Dad looked at me quizzically, as if to say, "Who is this kid?" Ax looked like any ordinary, slightly awkward junior high schooler. Maybe a little better-looking than average. After all, he did carry my DNA.

"It's okay, Dad. Remember? You met Ax once a while back and you thought he was weird then, too. That's just because he's really an Andalite. Elfangor's younger brother. Show him, Ax."

Dad waved his hand. "No, no. It's all right. I remember now. I've heard all about you. . . ."

But Ax was already morphing back to his true form. Stalk eyes sprang noisily from Ax's head. His mouth sealed into a smooth stretch of blue skin. A glistening tail blade grew up over his head. An extra set of legs shot out of his rear.

Dad gawked in amazement.

"Catching flies?" I said.

He closed his mouth and blinked a couple of times. "I just can't believe it."

I think all science types secretly believe in aliens. First Erik, then Ax. Dad had to be pleased.

<How far have you progressed toward Z-space penetration?> Ax asked.

"Uh, well, we successfully detected the sub-stellar background radiation with a working pro-totype last month. The phase shift we measured was in precise conformation with our theories. We are, I mean were, about to attempt a pulsed-clump transmission."

That seemed to interest Ax. It seemed to give me a headache.

<That's the very simplest form of subspace transmission, analogous to early human radio transmission using Morse code.>

"Exactly."

<If the pulsed-clump transmission is suc-cessful, full-spectrum communications will be a simple extension of the work.>

"Learn how to crawl before you walk," I com-mented to no one.

"There's one very large obstacle," Dad said. "We'll never be able to acquire the necessary equipment and components. They're not the sort of things you can pick up at Radio Shack."

<I like Radio Shack.>

"Sure," Dad said, "so do I. But they don't sell stellar coordinators. Maybe these Chee creatures could help us."

<The Chee cannot participate or assist in the transfer of technology that could enable war and destruction,> Ax explained. <It is written into their programming.>

"Then there's no hope," Dad said, leaning back against the tree.

"Dad, Dad, Dad. You underestimate your son. Burglary — in the name of justice and freedom, of course — is among the great variety of talents the Animorphs possess. You want it, we can get it."

Dad looked disturbed. "Marco, you can't just . . ."

"Don't worry. We only take from Controller-run corporations and we'll find a way to make everything okay when the war's over."

"But that doesn't make it right."

"Dad, nothing is right anymore."

He was silent for a moment. Then he rose to his feet and looked at us.

"Well, then, boys. Let's get busy."

CHAPTER 11

"I can't wait to get away from those lunatics at the office." Dad stuffed a handful of underwear and shorts into the open suitcase on the bed. "I'm glad I had those sick days stored up. People get all crazy over some stupid piece of electronics that probably won't work anyway."

I was standing next to him, in his bedroom at home, helping him pack. Dad took his camera out of a drawer and tossed it in with the heap of clothes.

"So, Dad? When we get to Acapulco, can I rent a Jet Ski?"

"They pollute and make noise," he answered

63

as he folded a screaming Hawaiian shirt. "And they're dangerous. Do you want to be responsible for affecting your environment in a negative way?"

"No, I just want to fly through the water at fifty miles per hour and jump a ten-foot wave."

"We'll see," he said.

"Why can't we wait until Nora can get some time off? Why do we have to go away now?" I pressed.

"I told you already, Marco," he said, tossing a faded bathing suit into the bag. "Because I need to get away from work for a while. It's obvious that idiotic device I've been working on is important to somebody. God knows why! But I'm in danger because of it. Kidnapped and held prisoner by some nutbags in costumes? I don't need that kind of stress. Let someone else finish the project."

That was the last thing I heard my father say.

There was a terrific bang. The bedroom door burst off its hinges and four human-Controllers dressed as cops rushed into the room.

Dad froze and look puzzled.

And then four separate Dracon beams converged on the figure of one solitary human. For a fraction of a second I saw clothes, skin, hair, all of it vaporize, leaving a blackened carcass haloed in blinding light.

The body evaporated in a cloud of smoke. A charred scuff on the floor was all that marked the spot where Dad had stood.

Then all four guns pointed at the boy. At me, Marco. I didn't even scream as my own body disappeared in flames.

Because it wasn't really me. It wasn't my dad, either, the guy the Yeerks now thought was dead.

The Yeerks left and I began to demorph. I wanted to see the scene with my own eyes.

Watching it all through the distorted prism of cockroach vision, sensing and feeling it all from under the molding by the closet, had not been enough. My human body emerged from the insect.

"All clear," I said quickly. The curtains were still drawn closed. "Are you guys okay?" The hologram of Erek shimmered and disappeared. He was lying on the floor by the bed. Scorched and smoking.

But it was Mr. King I was really worried about, the Chee who had played the part of my dad. He'd been reduced to a clump of patchy holographic images. Beneath and between the weak projections of human body parts, I could see damaged circuitry. The elaborate mechanical frame was now nearly skeletal.

"His projection capacity has been severely damaged," Erek observed, coming closer.

"Can you fix it?" I said anxiously.

"I hope so. But I have to get him home first. His structural matrix is in obvious jeopardy."

"What about yours?"

"My systems are ninety-nine percent intact," he said easily. "Were the projections convincing? The program to simulate the destruction of you and your father?"

"Awesome," I said. "The Yeerks won't be looking for us anymore. I told Jake I'd do whatever it took to get them off our trail."

Erek helped Mr. King to his feet. I peered out the window through the slit in the drapes. A police car was parked out front. The four Yeerk executioners stood casually on the sidewalk, talking to Nora.

They knew her. She knew them.

A new aggressiveness controlled her movements.

It didn't take a math prodigy to figure out what that meant.

Nora had been taken.

The Controllers climbed back in the squad car and drove away with the lights flashing silently.

I got a sick feeling in my stomach. Not the

kind you get when you smell rotten milk. The kind you get when you want to cry, but the tears just won't come.

Nora had been a nice lady. Could I have saved her? Could anyone have saved her?

The Yeerks must have taken her away in the night, as Dad was begging me to let him return home to get her.

I'd known she was in danger and I'd done nothing.

That was wrong. What was worse is that a part of me had wanted her out of our lives.

My stomach squeezed tighter.

No. I hadn't wanted it to happen. No.

I thought about my father. Can a person take that kind of loss twice in a lifetime? The "death" of the person they love most? The one they eat breakfast with each day? The one they sleep next to each night?

No. It would break him, the way losing Mom had.

"Come on," Erek said.

Nora pulled out of our driveway, following the Controller cops in her own car.

Erek and a barely concealed Mr. King, his android form breaking out all over, hobbled out of the bedroom and down the stairs.

"Can I help?"

Erek laughed.

"Can you bench-press five hundred pounds? He's mostly dead weight."

"Oh," I said dejectedly. "Okay. I'll get the door. How will you two make it home?"

"I'll project a hologram around us, an image of something slow-moving. I do a pretty good garbage truck."

The two Chee stumbled onto the back deck. I glanced back into the family room.

My eye caught a photo tacked to the cork board over my father's worktable. It was a snapshot of me and Dad, taken by Mom on a sun-drenched day several years ago.

Suddenly, reality hit.

I was dead. And this was the end . . . of school, of dates, of video games. Of everything normal.

The kid in that photo had prepared his last frozen pizza dinner. Had gone to his last math class. Had seen his last movie at the Cineplex.

That kid would never even hang out in his own backyard again. Because this wasn't his home anymore. He had no home.

He'd made the necessary sacrifice.

I could take the photo with me. It was small enough to fit in the beak of the osprey I would morph to fly away.

I took two steps toward the cork board, then stopped.

No.

I had my memories.

They would have to be enough.

CHAPTER 12

"*Akka upe ozo oti. Scule! Muta pule.*"

Ax looked at me hopefully.

<Is the translator chip working yet?>

"Uh, no. Not unless *muta pule* means something to you. Let's see . . . nope. Nothing."

Ax's eyes drooped and he turned back to the contraption they had been working on for the past few days.

Few *long* days, I would add. You should try spending your nights under a tree at Chee Park with a dog for a pillow.

The Chee tell some great stories about the last ten centuries. Kings, conquerors, explorers, that kind of thing. Mr. King was the cook on Dar-

70

win's ship and Henry Ford's production chief. I mean, that's very cool stuff. Fascinating stuff.

But honestly, without HBO, life gets a little scary.

"*Kino ala ozo* nev . . . nev . . . never catch them unless we know they're coming . . . *nem zurka kakis loti.*"

"Ax! Hey, for a second there, that was English. You did it."

<No,> Ax said quickly. <I am unable to stabilize the programming of the translator chip.>

He glanced at my dad.

"Could you couple it with this?" Dad lifted a blue wire, then pointed to a green, circular component.

<That would take time,> Ax said. <I should just interpret. Or attempt to summarize.>

Ax had been sifting interplanetary chatter for hours. And for hours we'd been gathered with him, all of us, in Ax's scoop. We'd come for the unveiling of the Z-space transponder. Dad hadn't mentioned it was still under construction.

"So, it doesn't even translate?" Rachel said impatiently. "What does it do?"

Ax stopped working and looked at us with his main eyes. He put a delicate hand on either side of the device. It was fairly small. Mini-cooler size.

But it was clear from the way Ax held it that it meant more to him than an icebox. He cradled it like a newborn baby. Wires dangled like legs. Incomprehensible cosmic chatter streamed softly from its earpiece.

<The transmission capacity is not yet enabled. Neither is the translator. But this device can monitor unscrambled Yeerk communications, which I have been doing for some time now.>

"Ax, you're amazing," Cassie said.

Ax looked at Dad and flashed one of his eye-smiles.

<At times you humans truly scare me,> he muttered softly. <A mere four decades from first orbital spaceflight to the discovery of Zero-space communication?> He stamped the dirt with a hoof for emphasis. <We Andalites may wish we had left you to the Yeerks.>

"So far you Andalites *have* left us to the Yeerks," Rachel pointed out dryly.

Ax could have countered the insult. But I think he was still torn between the pride of creation and the humiliation of learning that humans — that my father — had, in one huge intuitive leap, created a device that was in some ways superior to Andalite technology.

"Ax, what've you heard?" Jake said.

<It is very difficult to piece together,> Ax said

tentatively. <My knowledge of Yeerk culture is not great. I do not fully understand the nuances of Yeerk communication.>

<Don't worry, Ax-man.> Tobias, from a perch in a nearby tree. <What do you think they've been saying?>

<But I would be speculating. Guessing,> Ax protested.

"Go for it," Rachel ordered. "Live dangerously. If you don't, I'm leaving."

<There is one thing,> Ax began. <One very disturbing conclusion that I can draw, though with limited certainty.> Ax looked at me. <Visser One has returned to Earth. But for a grim purpose. She is being held at the Yeerk pool. She is to be executed as a traitor.>

I felt my body stiffen, my heart stop.

"Marco, Eva is Visser One," Dad said, his voice quaking.

I nodded.

<From what I understand,> Ax continued, <death as a traitor means death by Kandrona starvation. The event awaits only the necessary witness from the Council of Thirteen, who will arrive in two days. Visser Three will then be elevated to the post of Visser One. And,> Ax added, <there are rumors — nothing concrete, but suggestions — that the execution of Visser One is part of an overall change affecting Earth.>

I knew what that meant. We all did. Visser One, originator of the Yeerk invasion of Earth, favored a slow infiltration of Earth, a quiet, stealthy assault.

But Visser Three, a jumped-up egomaniac, has pushed for all-out conquest from the beginning. His dearest dream is to annihilate human power centers in an *Independence Day*-style war. To drive large numbers of humans into infestation camps. To do it quickly and publicly.

If he gets his way, the Animorphs won't matter. Everything will be lost. Millions will die. Human culture will be pulverized.

<Of course, this is only speculation,> Ax reiterated.

I laughed bitterly. "Ax, your speculations are like computer computations. This is more than a good guess."

"It can't happen," Jake said, his voice hard. "We can't let Visser Three get promoted. If Yeerk forces change their tactics — if they decide to go public — it will be the end."

What could I say? I'd just risked everything — every one of us — to pull my father out of trouble. I couldn't argue now for a mission to save my mother. The situation was different, far more dangerous.

It meant a trip to the Yeerk pool.

And then Cassie's voice, sounding clear and

innocent. And persuasive. "If Ax can't be sure what the Yeerks are planning, there's only one person who would be."

She was taking me off the hook. She was giving me the chance I couldn't ask for.

Every muscle in my face tensed until it hurt. I would not cry. I just wouldn't again forget that, in some ways, Cassie is the bravest and the smartest of my friends.

Still, I waited for someone else to speak. The image of my mother on death row, Yeerk prisoner, Yeerk victim, battered and beaten, bruised and broken, blazed in my mind's eye.

"Visser One," Jake said.

75

CHAPTER 13

I had to say something. Had to let them know I hadn't lost sight of the realities of this war.

"So what if Visser One is our best shot at finding out what Visser Three has planned? We risk our butts for her?"

Jake looked at me with eyes that said, "Give me a break. You know you want to save her."

"Listen!" I continued, more forcefully. "If we can rescue her — and that's a big if — she'll still have the Yeerk in her head. Why would it cooperate with us? Why would it tell us anything?"

"It won't," Jake answered simply, sinking my counterargument. "But we can starve it out."

"Is that painful?" Dad said anxiously. "Would she survive?"

"It's living hell," Jake answered. "But it would be more fun than anything she's been through so far."

Rachel glanced at Dad, then at me. "Where will your mom and dad go?" she said. "They'll have to leave the country. Get as far from here as they can."

"I can't do that," Dad protested. "I won't leave Nora."

"You don't have a choice," Rachel said coldly.

Another twinge of guilt struck me like a facial tic. Nora was probably the one Dad wanted to save. He could have left the country with her, his wife . . . been fugitives with the woman he loved . . .

<I know a nice place,> Tobias said. <Good climate, no tourists, low prices. Friendly locals. They're a little on the slow side, but they can tell a great story.>

"The free Hork-Bajir colony," Cassie cried. "We'll send them to the Hork-Bajir!"

It was the perfect solution to the problem of safety for my parents. Dad aimed a look of resentment at a far-off tree. An alien race of parasites had played god with his freedom. A bunch of kids had co-opted his free will. His life had

77

been totally taken over. He understood his new reality, but he didn't like it.

Did I? My mind flooded with sun-washed scenes of peace and harmony. Mom climbing a tree next to Toby. Dad teaching English in a flower-filled meadow. They could act as advisors for the Hork-Bajir. They could be unofficial governors of the valley. . . .

What was I thinking?

"Great idea," I said with mock enthusiasm. "Except it assumes that we make it out of the Yeerk pool death trap." I frowned. "Look, our odds for success might be pretty good in a world where Rachel is short, fat, and ugly, and Tobias is a stork. But in this world? We've used up most of our nine lives, kids. The Yeerks have got to have beefed-up security forces to prevent Visser One's escape. The odds are worse than slim."

"They're dim," Dad echoed. "And grim." I glared at him. Okay, so maybe we try to rhyme with each other's last word. But we do that when we're alone.

Dad smiled at the ground. A peace offering. I tried to finish my argument.

"What I'm trying to say is that we don't have a plan. We don't even know how to get into the pool anymore. Not since they closed the car wash."

<That's not true,> Ax said, glancing up with

his main eyes. He tuned a big knob on the Z-space transponder, then another, littler one. He removed the earpiece from his ear.

<I have heard enough Z-space communication to know that the Yeerks have recently added a major tunnel to the pool.>

<Where?> Jake said.

<Unclear. But it connects to a new underground facility for docking and repairing Bug fighters. The tunnel also carries out a complex decontamination process equipped to kill any living thing.>

"Ax," I said. "Last time I checked, we can't morph inanimate objects like chairs and tables. And if we could, they wouldn't stand much of a chance against a pack of Hork-Bajir."

"What about tiny animals?" Cassie suggested. "Would a flea or a fly be less susceptible to decontamination?"

<No,> Ax said with certainty. <Yeerk decontamination is thorough and effective.>

"Then why are you telling us this?" Rachel exploded.

<A Bug fighter's shield is sufficiently strong to block decontamination,> Ax suggested gently.

Jake smiled, an engaged yet tentative grin.

"I get it," he said. "All we have to do is steal a Bug fighter, find the new tunnel, fly through it, land in the docking facility, evade security, make it to the main pool, kidnap Visser One, drag her back to the ship, and escape. It's all so simple."

Rachel looked happier now that there was the promise of danger.

Cassie raised an eyebrow thoughtfully.

Tobias fluttered to ground level, giving me the impression that he supported this madness.

"You'll have to lay a trap for the Yeerks," Dad said suddenly. "If I've followed this debate correctly, you need a reaction large enough to bring in a Bug fighter, but small enough to give you some control."

I looked at him. My father never ceased to amaze me. Neither did the resilience of the human spirit.

"Dad's catching on," I said approvingly. "We do need a trap and I've got me an idea."

CHAPTER 14

"Can you hear me? Can you hear me? Is this the po-leese? I'm calling from the National Forest. I've got the darndest dang thing you ever did see trapped up here. It's some kind of monster with blades all over it."

Howls and groans echoed through the dark hills.

My friends?

Maybe.

Or maybe not.

The voice on the other end of the cell phone sounded like it was talking into a tin can.

It asked for clarification.

"Monster! Blades!" I cried. "I swear, I got me a real, live, outer-space alien!"

Instantly, I was headquarters' number-one priority. Where was I, they demanded? Who was I?

I gave my location, then cut the connection.

Spastic laughter gripped my chest. This plan was too insane! And I'd just set it in motion.

<Keep it down!> Jake roared from a shadow somewhere near.

I pulled a camouflaged hunting cap down over my head. This fashion statement was on loan from Jake's dad. It was supposed to shield my face so the Yeerks in the Bug fighter wouldn't recognize me as the boy gunned down the other day. The boy supposed to be dead.

"Let's hope this works," I whispered, fastening the earflaps under my chin and looking toward the sky.

A Bug fighter took exactly four minutes to swoop down from orbit. Its lights smeared a bloodred line across the sky. I crouched behind a massive pine tree. When the fighter passed low and slow overhead, I suddenly wished I'd snagged the hunting jacket, too.

Not the orange one.

The plan was for the Yeerks to see a cowering human — that would be me — attracted and repulsed simultaneously by the sight of a struggling Hork-Bajir, caught in some kind of leg trap.

Who was I to mess with the plan?

I cowered. Expertly.

I was glad Dad was safe at the Hork-Bajir colony. He had wanted a part in the mission. He'd been outvoted.

<They're coming in,> Rachel said. <They're going to land. Get ready!>

I fingered the coil of cable clutched to my chest. The fighter hovered lower and slower. Through the small, eyelike windows at the front, I saw a Taxxon at the controls.

Pshhhhhhh-shhhhh-thooomp!

The craft landed. A heartbeat later, a hatch slid open. Two Hork-Bajir jumped out, huge menacing shapes in the gloom of the forest.

Then — a tiger streaked from the utter darkness of the trees into the small clearing.

"Rrrrrroaaaaahhhhhh!"

WHAM!

One Hork-Bajir, knocked off his feet.

WHUMP!

A grizzly reared up and sideswiped the second warrior.

Craack!

That was his head, meeting the hull of the ship.

"*Gahh* . . ." he said softly. "*Lahh* . . ." Victim two. Knocked silly.

One more to go.

The Taxxon inside skittered hysterically from the controls to the hatch, and plunged onto the forest floor!

"Sneeet! Sneeyanyanahhhh!"

Look out! I screamed silently. Jake made me promise not to say a word. If the Yeerks thought a human was part of the attack, we'd be charred toast. All of us.

Yes! A wolf sprinted from the trees on the right. An Andalite streaked in from the left, a lightning line of blue.

Ploosh! Ploosh!

Cassie plowed into the Taxxon's rear half. Ax took the front.

The Taxxon was thrust into the night sky. A wormy constellation spinning clockwise at hyperspeed.

"Skreeeeeeeeyaaaaa!"

Ka-blooooosh!

He landed with a watery thud.

I ran toward the fighter. Tobias was already demorphing, growing smaller and smaller in the mantrap that held his Hork-Bajir leg. Once bird, he could wriggle free.

<Tie them up,> Jake ordered. <Just tight enough to keep them here till the free Hork-Bajir can pick them up.>

"What about the Taxxon?" I said.

<He can fend for himself. Maybe he makes it. Maybe he doesn't.>

"Right."

I wrangled two bladed Hork-Bajir arms into position and bound them together with cord. One of them groaned faintly, face in the dirt. Rachel silenced him with a flick of a great grizzly paw.

My heart was pounding wildly. But I managed to maneuver the legs and bind them. Then the hands and legs of the other one.

<Come on,> Jake ordered, demorphing.

Rachel climbed on board. Tobias flew in.

I looked down at the Hork-Bajir I'd just tied up. To the touch, the skin was rough as bark. His back heaved and fell. A sharp snort accompanied every intake of air.

I was going to the Yeerk pool.

And this breathing sawmill was going to be my costume.

CHAPTER 15

"How cool is this? This has got to be a limited edition sport model. I mean, wow. The Yeerks must only have made a few hundred of these."

I walked to one of the tiny windows. Red spotlights still crisscrossed the ground below, pulsing in deliberately slow cadence.

<Actually,> Ax corrected, <this is the standard model. Albeit the newest version.> His multifingered hands worked frantically to keep pace with controls made for the five hundred or so little claws of a Taxxon. <This model has been produced by the thousands.>

I watched Ax in profile as he worked furiously

to dim the searchlights. He was having some trouble. The cab lights went black, then red again. The outer lights brightened before they dimmed our RV-sized cockroach without legs.

Cockroach. The kind of thing that makes your mom frantically beat the wall with the kitchen broom and not want to eat for a whole day afterward.

A Bug fighter is not warm and fuzzy. It's not the kind of vehicle into which you want to crawl.

The sudden sound of compressed air being released . . .

"Ax?"

Whoooossshhhhhh!

"Aaaaaax!"

My head was thrown back. My body slammed against four other bodies on the cabin's back wall. A hawk screeched nervously as momentum plastered his bony body to the ceiling.

<I have control of the ship,> Ax said loudly. <Please remain calm. I think the cockpit was modified for a mutant Taxxon, a Taxxon with twice the normal number of appendages.>

I took a deep breath. Nice luck. Hijack a ship built for a mutant.

"Do you need help?" Jake asked.

"This is so stupid," I cursed under my breath.

From where I sat, helplessly pressed against

87

the bulkhead, Ax looked totally confused. His weak fingers ran over every button like a deranged pilot with a phantom checklist.

"Uh, Ax-man," I said, "do you have even, like, one little clue?"

<I now have several. I will need several more before I can pilot the craft effectively.>

Tobias fell to the floor with a thud. We'd stopped accelerating. Now we hovered indecisively.

Ax flipped two switches over his head, then pressed a red button. There was the sound of a fan. Warm air rushed out from under the seats that lined the sidewalls. Ax's stalk eyes swung around, puzzled.

"Much better, Ax," Rachel said impatiently. "You have the makings of a great heating-and-cooling engineer."

"Maybe we should read the owner's manual?" Cassie.

<No. No, that will not be necessary,> Ax declared, newly confident. <I have an idea. Rather than search for the tunnel entrance based on clues from Z-space chatter, why not let the Bug fighter guide us? All low-level Yeerk combat ships are programmed to return to base automatically if flight begins to seem, um, erratic.>

"A safety precaution?" Cassie asked.

<No. A security measure. The Yeerks don't trust their own pilots.>

"Yeah, well, good for them. We need autopilot bad."

The ship jolted. It began to ascend rapidly, then pivot slowly. And suddenly, even though it was night outside, everything through the main windows appeared lit up bright as day. Yeerk night-vision technology.

I moved to the front of the ship to get a better view. Silly of me. If I'd waited a half-second longer, I wouldn't have had to walk.

The ship pitched forward and angled down toward the earth. Before we could yell, the six of us were trapped in a pile-on.

<You should always wear the safety restraints,> Ax scolded, struggling futilely to get four humans and an angry bird off him.

I pulled myself to my knees. Below us, through the night-vision windows, was the ocean, crashing whitecaps and heaving swells.

"Ax, are you sure everything's okay?"

"We're pointed straight for the water!"

<I . . . I . . .>

"Yeeeeeoooooooooowwwwwwwwwww!"

The scream was unanimous.

"OhhhhhhhhMyyyyyyyyyGoooooooodddd!!"

I was down! We shot Earthward like a bullet. Acceleration crushed my chest. Rachel's leg wedged against my neck.

I could feel the skin of my face pulled back by the force.

"Yaaaaahhhh!"

CHAPTER 16

"Yaaaaaaaaaah!"

Seconds from plunging us into the watery depths, the Bug fighter got a different idea.

It slowed, stopped, pivoted. And shot upward!

"Ahhhh! What's going on?"

Everyone but Ax and Tobias skittered and slid across the floor, back against the bulkhead.

<Perhaps . . .> Ax said shakily. <Perhaps we did not register sufficient velocity. If the ship intends to follow an underwater course, sufficient speed must be attained beforehand.>

"Underwater!"

<I believe so.>

"Won't that kill us?"

<At these velocities, death is always a possibility.>

Great. Killed by autopilot. Totally humiliating death.

Then — the image of my mother popped into my head, as I'd seen her in the Yeerk pool, at the trial. Bones broken and body bloody. She'd asked for more of the Yeerks' cruelty. Begged me to let Visser One continue to control her. Because she knew it might give Earth a better chance for survival.

If she could take that kind of torture, I could deal with being at the mercy of autopilot.

I glanced out one of the windows. Ocean and forest and city lights were dropping away, like a high-speed pan-out from a satellite camera. For just an instant, I could make out the dots of lights that were the city. The stadium, the business district, the 'burbs, and the boonies.

Whooosh!

Then we pulled away so fast, all light converged into one bright dot, one speck of city. More dots came into view, until I could see hundreds of beacons of blazing white light. For a second, I thought they were stars. Then I realized that each one was a city. We were almost in outer space!

Cassie gasped. It was unbelievable.

<We should reach the apex of our trajectory at

any moment,> Ax said, inappropriately calm. <It would be wise to fasten your safety restraints.>

Again, the ship slowed. You couldn't feel g-forces anymore, but the earth below stopped receding. It was like we'd reached the end of some massive, invisible rubber band.

I'd shot off too many rubber bands during math class not to know what would come next.

Was I distressed?

Yes. Oh yes, I was.

Fwooop!

The ship tilted into a dive and without a second's hesitation —

"Aaaaaahhhh!"

<Aaaaahhhh!>

Raced toward Earth. Faster. Faster!

We punched through the clouds, a millisecond of fog.

Then, the sparkle of the city. The curved coastline.

And the ship diving straight at the water!

A plain of blue and silver filled the cockpit windows. Growing clearer and sharper every second!

Shimmering waves . . .

Someone screamed again. And at that moment I saw death.

We've dived from planes, demorphed in mid-air, dodged Dracon beams, done all these things

93

and more at lightning-fast speed. But nothing, nothing compared to this.

Just a fraction of a second to know, not even to articulate, okay, you're about to die.

Rushing toward a blue wall of death at a million miles an hour!

"Ahhhhhhhhhhhhhhhhhhhhhh!"

<Ahhhhhh!>

Six screaming voices. A weird whooshing in my head.

And then I opened my eyes.

Schools of fish streaked through the Bug fighter's red lights.

I was alive. And we were under the water. The ship had become a submarine! Autopilot banked and steered some secret course known only to the enemy.

I looked at the others. Rachel held Tobias's hawk body loosely but protectively. Ax stood on wobbly legs. Jake and Cassie were clutching hands. No one said a word.

We dove deeper, into darker ocean depths.

Leveled out along the ocean bottom, skimmed across a topography more bizarre than anything on the face of the planet. A cavern disappeared beneath us. A mountain jutted into blackness overhead. A bright yellow sea creature fled in our wake.

And suddenly, our lights illuminated a massive obstruction. Jagged, angular, covered over with sea life and yet, a familiar sight.

<It's a ship.> Tobias.

Yeah, like what you see on a cable show. *Lost Ships of the Sea: Terror, Treasure, and Discovery.*

"Go Hork-Bajir," Jake ordered. "Now. We may not have much time."

We morphed. Six panting, muscular, seven-foot-tall, blade-wielding bodies made the Bug fighter a tight fit. But it was the morph for the job and I knew what to expect. Good eyes. Slow mind, a little apprehensive. Powerful body. Just one of hundreds, maybe thousands of slaves to the Yeerks.

No one would notice us. No one would know we were not Controllers. I hoped.

The ship banked automatically, just missing the side of the seafaring relic. We began to circle slowly above it.

The hull was gigantic, tipped on its side against the ocean floor. Large sections were broken off, plates of riveted steel scattered all around. A turret and three heavy guns protruded from the deck.

<World War Two,> Jake murmured. <It's a battleship.>

The Bug fighter circled once more, then set a course for the center of the sunken ship.

<Here we go again,> I yelled, throwing up my

95

bladed arms in disbelief. <Don't tell me we can fly through steel.>

We shot toward the hull. I decided not to close my eyes this time. What would be the point?

<The Z-space chatter,> Ax said suddenly. <There was the mention of a human ship. This is the entrance to the tunnel!>

Just as we were about to crash, the ship fractured. Just opened like a hinged box, revealing a long slit through the superstructure.

Dead fish and other sea creatures poured out from the battleship opening, swarming our windows.

<Intense radiation screens,> Ax explained. <They are not uncommon as protective devices for Yeerk battle stations. Living things are destroyed instantly.>

I swallowed hard.

We passed through the slit with inches to spare and were swallowed into featureless blackness.

The ship dove swiftly under the seafloor, through an underwater tube to the center of the earth.

Gradually, the walls of the tunnel changed from water to soil. From rock to concrete.

And suddenly, our Bug fighter and its Hork-Bajir crewmen pulled into an enormous, light-flooded cavern. Service hangars lined the walls of the dome-shaped space, as big as the main Yeerk pool. The floor was alive with Taxxon and Hork-Bajir crewmen streaming to and from docked fighters. Human-Controller maintenance workers buzzed from ship to ship in one-person pods.

A Blade ship was being serviced in what looked like a private hangar.

Our Bug fighter zoomed purposefully along a line of docked Bug fighters until it came to an empty stall.

We descended slowly and landed with a slight jolt.

<We have docked,> Ax said unnecessarily.

Jake stood up. <Let's go, guys.>

CHAPTER 17

Six Hork-Bajir backed down the debarkation ladder and stepped onto a hard concrete floor.

I, for one, was doing my best to look extremely mean.

<All these fighters,> Cassie said in private thought-speak. <The Yeerks have an amazing force!>

Yeah, the power assembled here was more than any of us had expected. Dozens of Bug fighters. A Blade ship. And these were just the ones in for servicing.

If the all-out invasion came, it wasn't going to be pretty.

<Stay calm, everybody,> Jake said. <Pretend you know where you're going. And look tough.>

98

Other Bug fighter crews marched across the mammoth room. We mimicked them by forming three rows of two and striding along until we neared a security checkpoint.

Two Dracon-slinging Hork-Bajir heavies looked us over carelessly. The third one, a thinner, savvier-looking guy, raised a bladed arm for us to halt.

If I'd been a normal kid, without the superhuman bravery of an Animorph, my heart probably would have stopped. It wasn't just the three security guards. I mean, the six of us could take them. It was the other hundred or so Hork-Bajir milling around. The complex was alive!

The thin security guard slid off his stool, walked up to Ax, looked him up and down. Then he backed away and snorted to the others.

"Grrraffshhh Grrrrufssshhhht!"

Finally, he waved us on.

<No, you have a nice day, sir,> I said softly. Nobody laughed. <Look, we might be in a Yeerk fortress, but life's about experience, right? This is experience.>

<Shut. Up,> Rachel said.

<Okay.>

We followed other crews to a long corridor at the edge of the cavern in which we'd parked the ship. There was a moving walkway, like the conveyer belts for people at the airport. In lanes on either side of us, transport vehicles raced in both directions.

<We're definitely headed for the pool,> Tobias observed.

<We'll have to split up to find Visser One,> Jake said. <The place is huge and we probably don't have much time.>

A few moments later we emerged from the connecting tunnel into the cavernous Yeerk pool complex we'd come to know and love.

And there, in the center of the sloshing pool itself, tied to a stake in the middle of the infestation pier, was Visser One.

My mother.

<That was easy,> Cassie said.

Visser One — my mother — was roped and chained. If there was a part of her body that wasn't bruised or bleeding, I couldn't see it. It hurt just to look at her.

I wanted to run to her, cut her free. But didn't. It would have been suicide for all of us.

Controllers jeered and yelled at her from the side of the pool. She was no longer their visser. She was a traitor, a loser.

Torture, humiliation, death. The Yeerks had made the execution a public event.

And obviously, the starvation was well underway. The visser thrashed madly and screamed incomprehensible words at the crowd.

The Yeerk in my mother's head was desperate. Surrounded by Kandrona she couldn't have, starving in the midst of plenty.

A sick, retching feeling twisted my stomach.

<Mom!> I yelled in private thought-speak.

Her jabbering stopped abruptly. She'd heard my thought-speak. My mother was still alive enough to know my voice!

<Mom!> I yelled again. This time, she didn't respond. Or couldn't. Visser One reasserted control, roaring and wailing, spitting at her tormentors. Pulling at wrists and ankles bound tight and black with bruising. I had to look away.

A bladed claw pressed gently against my back. It was Jake.

<I know this is tough,> he said. <But we have to do it right.>

<Visser One knows who we are,> I said quickly. <In the state she's in, starved out of her mind, she could say anything.>

<Would anyone listen to her?> Cassie said. <Would anyone even understand?>

<She will not talk,> Ax said.

<What makes you so sure?> Tobias said.

<She has nothing to gain by telling them. She will die anyway.>

<True,> Tobias said thoughtfully. <But you could also argue that she has nothing to lose by telling them. I know what it's like. I know what it

does to you. If she thinks it might save her, she'll talk.>

<How can we get her out of here?> Rachel said practically. <We can't just pick her up and carry her all the way back to the ship.>

<Right,> I said, struggling to focus, to plan. <We wouldn't get two feet without being slaughtered. We are seriously outnumbered.>

<Okay, so the subtle rescue-and-escape plan is not happening,> Cassie said. <What . . . >

<Back to the ship,> Jake commanded. <Now.>

<And leave Visser One?> Cassie cried, indignant. <We've made it this far. We can't give up.>

<No one said anything about giving up,> Jake said.

He turned his fierce Hork-Bajir eyes toward the entrance to the connecting walkway. Scrutinized the channel through which we'd arrived at the Yeerk pool.

Ax was the first one to understand.

<I am an excellent pilot,> Ax said. <But as you have witnessed, Yeerk ships are not as responsive as Andalite craft. I do not think such tight confines are maneuverable.>

<We're going to fly her out?> Rachel said.

<Got a better plan?> Jake was already moving toward the walkway, back to the ship. We followed, walking quickly. Stepped onto the conveyer belt with a group of Taxxon pilots.

102

And then, as we approached the maintenance dome, a security force assembled.

<Please let them be there to question these Taxxons,> Tobias said.

"*Sttoooopflesshh!*" the lead security agent commanded.

Jake stopped.

<Keep walking,> he told us. <I'll handle this.>

"Your fighter is overdue. Explain!"

"Yes," Jake said, articulating human language sounds as clearly as a Hork-Bajir beak would allow. "We were cruishh . . . cruising over the forest when our right thruster stopped working. I had to land. My orders were to have the fighter maintenanced here."

<Stay cool, everybody,> he added privately.

"That's a lie," cried the thin Hork-Bajir from before, shoving Jake into his men. "There was a full system check. Nothing is wrong with your ship. *Gufleccccssshhhh!*"

Hork-Bajir from neighboring hangars craned their necks to see if there would be a struggle.

<On second thought,> Jake directed, <everybody, run!>

CHAPTER 18

Jake raised his bladed elbows and sliced into the wall of Hork-Bajir trying to restrain him.

Note to self: Do not attempt to contradict Yeerk security forces. It only leads to mayhem.

<Get to the fighter!> Jake screamed.

He punched another Hork-Bajir out of his way and raced down the long row of ships. Suddenly —

Tseeeeeew! Tseeeeeew!

The air around him exploded in a flash of Dracon fire!

<No!>

Jake disappeared in a cloud of glowing smoke.

<Jake!> Cassie screamed.

<Relax,> Jake called out to us, panting heavily. <I'm okay. I'm crouched behind a service trolley.>

He was out of sight, but that didn't mean security believed he was dead. All attention, all guns, all Dracon beams swarmed toward the smoky cloud where Jake had last been seen.

No one noticed the transformation that was taking place behind other conveniently placed pieces of equipment. A muscular blue Andalite and a red-tailed hawk, growing and morphing where two Hork-Bajir had stood seconds before. Tobias flapped up, high and silent, into the bowl of the dome.

Thwack . . . Thwack-Thwack-Thwack!

Ax!

"Aaghshs . . ." Four Dracon beams clattered to the ground. Four warriors clutching fingerless stumps let loose with desperate, confused cries.

Ax shot off like a bullet in Jake's direction.

Cassie, Rachel, and I, still in our Hork-Bajir morphs, grabbed the Dracon weapons off the floor.

<Fire at Ax!> I yelled.

It was our best chance, our only option for cover. As long as we shot at the Andalite, the Hork-Bajir wouldn't shoot at us. We ran after Ax. Missing every shot.

<Get to the ship!>

Bug ship crews were running for their fighters. We had no time!

Words to live by: When you're running from the enemy, don't look back. It never does any good. I turned around to see a stampede of angry, armed Hork-Bajir pouring through the connecting tunnel.

Did I need to see that? Was that good for morale? No. It was not.

"Traitors!" I raged suddenly, waving my Dracon beam toward a disorganized group of security Hork-Bajir. "Over there. Over there! Get them!"

"Guflesshhhkkl Defffantii!" cried the leader of the first wave. "Die, traitors!" Off they went. Security force against security force.

Exactly what we needed. Civil war. Confusion. Yeerk against Yeerk.

<Get your butts in the ship!> Jake roared. <I'm inside. I'm waiting!>

Where were Rachel and Cassie? I'd lost them. I was alone.

I ran.

My long, hard claws scratched the cold, hard floor. The Hork-Bajir heart pounded like a bass drum in my chest. Lungs burned. Sweat dripped into my eyes.

Our ship's bug-eye windows glowed red, powering up.

<All systems are go,> Ax said from inside. <Autopilot is disabled. I have full control.>

<Let's ride, Ax,> Jake ordered.

<Wait! For! Me!> I bounded up the narrow maintenance ladder and into our ride.

Ax was at the controls. Tobias was perched like a figurehead inside.

<Let's cruise for some chicks,> I breathed, already starting to demorph. <I lost the girls.>

We lifted off.

<Shields up,> Ax said.

Ka-Bammm! Dracon fire grazed our force-field bubble.

Ax didn't wait for further orders. He knew what to do.

We shot into the air. Dove down. Shot up again. I felt like I'd left my stomach in the maintenance hangar.

I was human now, morph-capable. I'd had enough of the Hork-Bajir. I wanted something hairy and familiar.

<There!> Tobias yelled. <I see them! Behind that maintenance pod.>

We rose again. Then, dipped. Rose, dipped. Bug-fighter frenzy: The carnival ride from hell.

Ax moved in and opened the hatch.

<Shields down,> he said.

Cassie was crouched low, shielding her head

from Dracon fire. I reached out with a still-forming gorilla hand. Grabbed hold. Pulled!

<Ahhh!>

Cassie was in.

Rachel tumbled through the hole after her.

<Shields up.>

Tseeew!

The maintenance vehicle exploded in a flash of heat that sent us rocking.

<Ax,> Jake ordered, <get us out of here!>

CHAPTER 19

I moved to a window. The red, bloodshot "eyes" of Bug fighters everywhere were coming to life.

One rose from its hangar, still tethered to the maintenance tubes and tools that clung to its hull.

It tried to accelerate.

Blaamm!

A white flash. An instant explosion.

<Do not attempt to fly a ship undergoing maintenance,> Ax counseled. <Something is bound to go wrong.>

<Yeah, well, we're not doing so hot ourselves,> I said.

Handheld Dracon fire battered our shields. Ax

pointed the ship at the connecting tunnel and slammed on the gas.

Wee-oo-wee-oo!

A deafening alarm! Flashing lights seized the controls. I looked at Ax.

<We do not have clearance. Too narrow.>

<Do something, Ax!> Jake cried.

Ax did. He slowed the ship, turned our Dracon cannon on the rock of the connecting tunnel, and fired. Solid rock began to burn and melt and disappear!

Tobias was monitoring the shields. <Shield strength is fading, Ax! Twenty-eight percent. Twenty-six!>

The stone blazed. Chunks of smoldering, flaming cliff crashed onto the conveyor belt we'd walked across minutes before.

Ka-Bam! Bamm! Bam, bam, bam!

Dracon fire continued to rock us from below.

<Ax! Can you fly us through, yes or no?>

<Yes.>

<Whoa!>

The ship banked forty-five degrees! And Ax took us into the flames. Scraping . . . bumping . . . screeching through the exploding rock!

We were like a bullet in a gun barrel.

<Ax, you're craaaaazy!> Cassie screamed.

Suddenly, light. Air.

The gigantic Yeerk pool complex opened up before us.

<Nice work, Ax-man,> Jake said, breathing hard. <Now, let's take their minds off Visser One.>

He aimed the Dracon cannon at a complex of outbuildings on the edge of the pool. Fired. Missed!

<Let the master take over.>

I took the controls.

Tseeeew!

An outbuilding disappeared. Another erupted in flames.

Tseeeew!

An unmanned earthmover vaporized. Controllers scattered in all directions. It was a Hollywood summer weekend movie.

I ruled.

I turned the cannon on the pool.

My mother might have been delirious, but her eyes went wide at the sight of the training cannon.

<Careful,> Rachel said.

I aimed at the edge. Not at the Yeerks, not at the Controllers. Just at the thick metal tank. The symbol of enslavement.

Tseew!

A low-power burst made the tank wall melt.

No major damage because I wasn't trying to destroy it. I was just trying to get everyone to run.

Hork-Bajir and humans fanned out in a desperate escape.

<Take us in,> Jake said to Ax. <Rachel, Marco? You ready?>

I snorted. <If we can't do it, no one can.>

<Let's do it!>

Ax hovered the ship above the Kandrona slop. The under-hatch opened.

<Shields down,> Ax said nervously.

<Go!> Jake yelled. <Go!>

We jumped out. Gorilla feet and Hork-Bajir talons slammed onto the metal peninsula where my mother was tied up. The infestation pier is as wide as a boardwalk, but it's as dangerous as a rope bridge strung across a canyon in the Andes.

Rachel quickly sliced the cuffs that held my mother to the pole. Chest . . . wrists . . . ankles.

My mother didn't seem to know we were there to help. The screaming Yeerk in her head was too far gone.

<Grab her,> Rachel growled. <The ship's about to get hit!>

Tseeeew!

A Dracon bolt hit the ship over our heads! The force rattled the pier and burned a scar into the side of our fighter!

<Hang on!> Jake called from above. <We'll be back.>

No choice. Ax had to pull away or be massacred. The ship raised its shields and buzzed into the air.

<We're stranded,> Rachel said. <This isn't how it was supposed to work out!>

Another Bug ship zoomed through the connecting tunnel, swarmed the air over the pool. Ax shot straight up to the top of the dome, the attacking ship right behind.

Tseeew!

Dracon fire missed Ax as he pulled steeply back.

Tseeew!

Jake shattered the shield of the enemy ship.

I turned back to my mother, leaned low to protect her body from the fight. <Mom, it's me. It's Marco.>

Carefully, I lifted her into my arms. She was silent for less than a second, then the screaming started again.

Tseeew! Tseew!

<Duck!> Rachel yelled. Stray fire from the aerial fight was dislodging pieces of rock from the ceiling! Small boulders rained to the floor like deadly hail.

Ka-plash! Ka-plash-plash-plash!

Chunks splashed into the pool, feet from us, covering us is a spray of goo.

<We're in trouble now,> Rachel said solemnly, pointing to a fearsome-looking group of Hork-Bajir marked with blue armbands on their bulging biceps.

<Who are those guys? They're . . . huge. Crap. They're the most pumped Hork-Bajir I've ever seen!>

I threw my kicking, fighting mother over my shoulder.

<Let's get to the other pier!> I shouted.

<Then what?>

<Run like hell.>

The gap between the piers was at least five feet. Maybe more. Rachel ran down our pier like it was an airstrip. She lifted up . . . rocketed through space . . .

The perfect long jump.

<Marco, come on!>

No choice. I taxied like a DC-3. The jump was too long, too . . .

<Ahhhhh!>

We hurtled through the air above the churning Yeerks.

And crashed onto the reinfestation pier.

Suddenly, my mother went totally limp.

Oh, God. Was she dead? Had I killed her?

No. Her eyes fluttered open and she looked at me pleadingly.

"Kill it," she whispered.

What? I looked down on the pier.

Visser One! The overgrown leech had escaped from my mother's ear and was trying to bail! It must have tried to drop into the Kandrona that was food, that was life. . . .

Trouble was, the timing of the jump had been off. Visser One had hit the pier as we landed.

And now it was wriggling away.

am!

A blue-banded Hork-Bajir slashed Rachel in the face!

Bam! Bam, bam, bam!

She struck back, a kickboxing, blade-slashing frenzy. The Hork-Bajir staggered, but stayed on his feet.

"I am Grath," he growled, eyes yellow-orange infernos. "I am the leader of the elite Blue Band Squadron. You will surrender or you will die."

<Surrender?> Rachel said to me, incredulous. <He doesn't know me very well.>

"A Hork-Bajir's gonna die on this pier, Mr. Grath," she snarled. "But it's not gonna be me."

Whooosh!

"Kill it!" My mother's voice rose louder now, trembling with anger. Visser One was crawling, shriveling up to half its size, then stretching forward. Shrivel, stretch. Shrivel, stretch. A slow, relentless rhythm toward the pier's edge.

I reached to grab it . . .

Bam!

<Ahhh!>

A claw-foot stabbed my leg! Another Hork-Bajir had landed on the pier!

I dropped my mother in a heap.

"You will die, Andalite!" Another Blue Band jabbed my back!

BAM!

I whirled and punched him in the chest. <I don't think so, freak.>

I glanced down to where my mother lay motionless, semiprotected between Rachel and me, oblivious to the battle. Bruised and broken, she was barely able to lift her head.

But still, she raged. "You won't get away, filthy worm!"

Tseew! Tseewtseew!

<Ahhh!> Rachel cried. <I'm hit! Bad.>

Had to help Rachel!

"Kill it!"

Had to help Mom!

I clenched my fist, a gorilla wrecking ball. I brought it up, ready to slam it down on the slug.

Tseeew!

"AAAAaaarghhhh!"

Searing pain raced through my right leg!

I dropped to the pier, clutching burns so painful I couldn't think. The smell of my own burning hair and flesh filled my nostrils, sweet and sickening. . . .

<Marco!> Rachel.

"Kill it!" My mother.

Insane fighter combat in the air overhead! More rock raining down!

Bam!

The Blue Band slashed me on the face.

Okay. That was unnecessary.

Rage drove me to my feet.

Ka-bam!

"Galaaaah!"

I punched Blue Band off the pier.

Splash!

He flailed, struggled in the muddy sea. . . .

A Bug fighter buzzed my head. The wake of air pushed me down. The roar of engines filled my ears, a shrill, deafening whine.

Then, without warning —

TSEEEEW!

A red flash over our heads.

Ka-BLAAMMM!

The Bug fighter blew apart, showering us with fiery debris!

Mounds of guts and severed limbs every-where!

<No!>

Jake, Ax, Cassie, Tobias . . . gone!

All gone.

<Noooooooooooo!>

Rachel!

I spun around, jumped over Mom. Smashed into the two warriors that pinned Rachel to the pier.

The anger was overwhelming. The pain nau-seating.

Whoomf! Bam!

I slammed my pile-driver arms into the Hork-Bajir chests. The bodies rolled, splashed . . .

<Come on! Let's move!> I shrieked.

My head was reeling. Rachel's left arm was a vein and a skin flap from falling off. My mother was helpless. Two more bladed Blue Bands were clanging down the infestation pier, gaining speed to make the jump . . .

Suddenly, the dome went eerily quiet.

The other Bug ship had disappeared. No roar of engines. No Dracon weapons firing. No battle.

A new sound . . .

119

The sound of laughter, mind-filling, evil thought-speak laughter, flooding the pool complex.

The Blue Bands froze in their tracks.

I looked across the pool. Visser Three stood on the shore, his stolen Andalite head tilted back.

Then, he began to morph.

The blue Andalite body turned black. Long, flat appendages sprouted from his neck and back, then opened outward in both directions, forming wings. Huge black wings!

Growing fuller and wider till they joined in the center. A continuous delta wing. A living stealth bomber.

A head grew in the middle. No, not a head . . .

A mouth! Wide and long and lined with a darting silver tongue that licked rows of shimmering teeth.

Then eyes . . . orange globes big as softballs, flanking the mouth like hardened gobs of tomato sauce.

<Haa, haa, haa,> he squawked. <Poor little Andalites. Abandoned on the pier. Abandoned to die. . . .>

The massive wings undulated only once, but it was enough to make the visser rise into the air. A second wing flap and he soared toward the top of the dome, an enormous silhouette engulfing us in shadow.

<Meet the *Bievilerd*!> the visser roared. <A little something I picked up on the planet Ondar. Its teeth will shred your flesh like paper.>

Rachel and I were silent. What could we say to that?

<You will die!> the visser cried. <And everyone here will see me kill you!>

<We have to move!> I yelled to Rachel.

<I can't,> she said.

<You have to!>

But I knew it was impossible. A river of blood gushed from her severed arm. She was losing consciousness.

Visser Three closed up his wings and dove for the pier, a missile with a mouth.

There was no escape. No escape!

I tried to lift both Rachel and my mother. They shuddered and gasped with pain. My attempt was pathetic! My injuries made me too weak to do anything. . . .

Suddenly —

Zzeeeeoowwwwww! A Bug ship zoomed out from behind a storage building!

Tseeew!

A Dracon blast, right into the *Bievilerd*'s belly.

"Rooooaaaaahhhhhhhhh!"

The visser shrieked. The fighter rocketed to-ward us.

<Marco!> It was Jake's voice . . . Jake's fighter!

<But I saw you crash!>

<No,> he said. <You saw the Yeerks crash. Where's your faith in the Ax-man? Hang on, we're coming in.>

CHAPTER 21

Tseeew!

A second hole sizzled the *Bievilerd*'s folded wing. It crumpled, wilted, crashed . . .

<Andalite filth!> the visser screamed. <You will pay. I will make you pay! Kill them!>

Tseew! Tseew!

Jake took out the two remaining Blue Bands just before we were sliced in their mobile Cuisinart-of-war.

<I'm losing it, Jake,> Rachel mumbled, still fallen close by. <You have to get us out of here!>

I tried to lift my mother again, but this time she resisted, summoning all her feeble strength.

Dracon strafe sprayed the pier. . . .

"Die!" she wheezed, eyes fixed on a small gray spot an inch from the edge.

Visser One!

<Mom, stop!>

She fell forward, arm extended, clutching . . .

"Die!"

The Bug ship flew in over the pool, blocking us from Dracon fire, hovering low just feet away.

My mother's face was distorted. Real human tears ran from her cheeks. Rage, pain, joy . . .

And then her hand squished the parasite.

But the slug was still alive. . . .

"No!"

I slammed my foot on the still-wriggling worm. And it was clear . . .

. . . it was clear that Visser One's journey had ended.

My mother, Eva, looked into my gorilla eyes with an expression of sick satisfaction. In spite of everything, it scared me.

"Now we can go," she whispered.

Then she fainted in my arms.

Ax lowered the shields. I jumped on board. Jake and Cassie leaped out, lifted Rachel, and set her inside. The operation took longer than it should have. . . .

<The ship is hit!> Cassie yelled.

<It can't be!> Tobias said.

<Ax?>

We dropped. The engines died like we'd pulled the plug.

Ka-PLASSSSH! We smashed into something . . . soft . . . something fluid.

Glug-glug-glug!

Ax's nimble fingers worked frantically on the controls. I moved to a window.

<We're in the POOL!> I cried.

Cassie coaxed Rachel through her demorph to repair near-fatal injuries. I had to do the same.

<Prince Jake, I cannot regain takeoff velocity. The pool is like a bog. The more we move, the more it sucks us under.>

We were slowly sinking into the heart of enemy territory!

I slammed a human fist against the cabin wall.

Saw that my mother's eyes were open. Saw that she was trying to speak but could produce nothing but a scratchy, phlegmy sigh.

"Mom, what is it?"

She looked up at Ax.

"Send the Dracon beam supply into overload," she muttered.

"What?" I said. "Ax, did you hear that? She said to send the beam supply into overload."

Ax turned his stalk eyes.

<That will explode the ship. It will destroy us.>

"Ax, listen to her!"

<Does your mother wish to see us die?> Ax said privately.

"Ax, she's free now," I said. "She's free!"

"It won't explode the ship," she went on, gagging with the effort. "Not if you time it right. When the Dracon power supply reaches one hundred fifty-five percent of maximum, shunt it to the engines, then fire the beams to bleed off any overcharge."

I looked at Ax. Ax looked at Jake. Jake looked at Cassie, who was looking at a now-human Rachel.

<It makes sense — I guess,> Tobias said from his perch near the controls.

<Then do it,> Jake said.

<But . . .>

<Do it.>

The screaming sound of beam overload raged until even I thought the ship would explode.

But my mother had been a Yeerk host for a long time. She'd learned a few things. She knew what she was doing.

The screaming stopped. Ax fired the beams

directly into the pool. A cloud of smoke and steam billowed around us.

<What's going on?>

<Technically?> Ax answered. <Water molecules are exploding. Simplistically? We are boiling Yeerks.>

Cassie turned away from the window. The ship began to rise.

Ax punched the power.

In the background, Visser Three continued to roar. <You will die, Andalites! I will kill you slowly and painfully! You are mine!>

We zoomed through the burned-out connecting walkway. Blew through the docking area, the repair facility, and into the tunnel. Yeerk fighters were on our tail.

I knelt next to my mother. Took her into my arms as we erupted into the sea. Cradled her gently, securely.

The Bug fighter punched through the ocean surface and into the night sky. Then up, up into the atmosphere.

Ax's voice came as a distant alarm.

<We are outnumbered, Prince Jake. Ships are dropping from orbit to attack.>

<No choice,> Jake answered. <Ditch the ship.>

Immediately, the ship turned, dove, plummeted toward the National Forest.

127

We crash-landed and bailed seconds before Bug fighters shot up the wreckage.

Not far from the place in the woods where this adventure had begun. We were almost back at our starting point.

Only this time, I had a prize.

CHAPTER 22

"Mom?"

"Yes, sweetheart?"

She put her hand on my shoulder and looked into my eyes.

Her own eyes had healed up pretty well. The scars on her face and arms, the broken bones, the bruised tissue . . . Nature had done a good job.

First aid from the Chee hadn't hurt, either.

She looked just like she used to. Well, almost.

The change was nothing obvious. It was a sort of tension, a vigilance in her face. It hadn't been there when I was younger.

Because she hadn't been a slave before.

A golden sun warmed the sky. Fluffy, non-threatening clouds dotted the blue.

129

A perfect day. But if it was a perfect day, why didn't I feel perfect? If this was my dream come true, why did I feel so wrong?

We were footsteps from the valley of the Hork-Bajir, the Promised Land for refugees. So why did I feel uneasy?

"Sweetheart, what is it?" Mom said again.

"Nothing. Just that this valley is awesome. You're going to be safe. Free. And I'm glad, that's all."

We crested the hill and the full effect of the valley spread out before us.

Standing on the rim of the Grand Canyon? Same kind of feeling.

Mom was visibly impressed.

"The Yeerks have no idea. They think they destroyed all this." She darkened suddenly. "And they will yet. Visser Three will have force enough to launch his attack in just a few months. He'll burn cities from orbit, Marco. He'll enslave the human race."

She had been Visser One. Who was I to argue with her predictions?

"Yeah, well, maybe not," I said bravely. Being brave is my job.

A waving hand caught my eye. Down the slope, near a group of Hork-Bajir flashing blades in welcome, was one smiling human.

130

Dad.

I didn't say anything. Neither did my mother. She just took off down the slope like a woman who hadn't seen her husband in months and months and months. . . .

It was a movie cliché. It was lovers reunited. It was the dream I'd had ever since I knew my mother was alive. Dad opened his arms and she tumbled into them.

They embraced. They held each other for a long, long time.

Everything I'd worked for was right before my eyes.

So what was this heaviness pressing on my heart?

The Hork-Bajir had prepared a feast. Bark Wellington. Bark Schnitzel. Bark chow mein. Bark fumé à la crème.

As I unpacked the supermarket cans I'd brought along, I assured the Hork-Bajir it's the thought that counts.

I'd forgotten a can opener, but who needs one in the valley of the walking Swiss Army knives?

The sun began to set as we finished our dinner. The Hork-Bajir lighted their campfires. Mom listened intently as Jara Hamee started one of his now-famous stories.

Dad pulled me aside.

"Marco?" he said in a whisper. "Was there any way to save Nora? Is there any way to save her now?"

His words made me feel a little sick. But by now, I knew that life, and love, were complicated.

"You know that I love her —"

I nodded. Made the decision.

"Dad, what if Nora was a Controller all along? What if the Yeerks put her in your path because they knew you were involved in secret work?"

Pain knotted my father's face.

My conscience was heavy. Permanent damage had been done. My family was back together, but not really.

Not honestly.

It was a desperate speculation, one that, I hoped, would make it easier for my dad.

It didn't make it any easier for me.

"What are you saying?"

"You were set up by the enemy," I said. "You can't blame yourself."

CHAPTER 23

The waves lapped at the sandy shore.

<Three miles,> Tobias called down. <The closest humans are three miles down the beach. But I don't think they're going anywhere. They're, um, pretty focused on each other.>

Not that I could see the waves. It was night, with an unhelpful crescent moon.

"This thing is really ready?" Jake asked, looking down at the infamous Z-space transponder.

We'd let a little time pass. Not much. Just enough to let Ax finish the device.

<Ready for transmission, Prince Jake. The translator chip has been installed and enabled.>

Jake smiled. Gave me a not-so-inscrutable

look of . . . a look that acknowledged our friend-
ship under fire.

Dad and I had been reported gunned down by
unidentified intruders. The local police had no
leads. No clues.

No surprise.

The investigation was underway. A lie that
made the neighbors feel better.

Nora was a casualty, one more Controller in
our midst. She still lived at the house, still
taught at my old school. Tobias spotted her one
night loitering around a known Yeerk pool entrance.

Maybe . . . maybe someday I could save her.

Chee Land wasn't so bad. That's where I
stayed now, mostly. They had TV. They had Oreos.

When I needed a cable fix, I spent the night
at Ax's scoop. It was too risky for me to be at
Cassie's or Rachel's or Jake's.

And when we didn't have a mission, I went to
the valley.

Always to the valley.

"Let me go over this one more time," I said.
"Transmission may mean interception by the
Yeerks, so we have to be careful what we say. And
we can't hang around when we're done. Ax takes
the machine with him so the Yeerks can't track
us to this transmission site."

"Wait," Rachel interrupted. "Can't we encrypt the transmission? Like they do in the movies?"

<It will be encrypted, in four separate pathways,> Ax said with a hint of disdain. <But to Yeerk cryptographic equipment, the disguise is elementary.>

"But there's a chance?" Cassie said hopefully. "A chance they'll think the signal is coming from one of their own ships?"

<A small chance,> Ax answered.

"Let's do this," Jake said, rubbing his hands together.

"Let's hope the fleet is open twenty-four hours," I said. "Ax, you've got the Andalites on your speed dial, right?"

I shifted my feet anxiously in the sand. Breathed deeply.

Ax typed a line or two of code on the abbreviated keypad. His fingers trembled slightly. This was a long-distance call.

I glanced at the sky, into the sea of stars and planets and alien worlds that lay beyond my view.

"Look!" Cassie said, pointing to a small dome-shaped light on the side of the machine that glowed a regal blue.

<We have a connection,> Ax said.

All four of his eyelids blinked rapidly. His posture straightened.

A voice . . . a scratchy, commanding voice . . .

<Who is this?> demanded the Andalite officer on the other end. <Who is initiating this contact?>

It was surreal! This voice . . . these words . . . Our link to another world!

Jake signaled Ax to answer.

But Ax shook his head.

<No. I believe this is your moment.>

Jake glanced at each of us, ran his hand through his hair.

"This is . . ." He cleared his throat. He glanced back at Ax and smiled. Then he leaned in close to the device.

"This is Earth," he said.

We do know who they are . . .

and we know you, too . . .

#46 The Deception

Tobias kept careful watch from above. Marco hung over my shoulder.

And with the aid of Cassie's cell phone and my new, lime green iMac, I proceeded to reroute the Yeerk Z-space transmissions through the NSA's central computer.

"Federal prison," Marco said, "here we come."

<What's happening, Ax?>

I related the sequence of events as they occurred.

<The NSA is attempting to block out my transmission. Now they are receiving our offering. My code-cracking program.>

A few keystrokes. A moment of tension. Waiting.

"Ax, what's going on!"

<The NSA have halted their efforts to keep me out. Now, let's see what we find.>

<One thing, Ax-man,> Tobias called. <Uh, are

you sure the program you sent these guys can't be used to deciper your own stuff? Or the Yeerks'?>

Slowly, I swung one eye stalk around and up to look at Tobias, perched on the branch of a tree.

<Okay, okay, sorry I asked.>

And then, suddenly, it happened.

This bigger, faster, more powerful machine, combined with my superior Andalite technical knowledge and skills . . .

". . . The newly appointed Visser One, recently Visser Three, current leader of the Yeerk mission on planet Earth . . . has approved Operation 9466. Visser Two has undertaken a journey to Earth to assist in the execution of this long-anticipated military action . . ."

"Bingo," Marco whispered.